4.0

THE LIBRARY CARD

Dear Arrow Teacher —

Happy Reading!

Jerry Spinelli

JERRY SPINELLI

THE
LIBRARY
CARD

SCHOLASTIC PRESS
NEW YORK

This presentation set of uncorrected galley sheets
of Jerry Spinelli's *The Library Card* has been prepared
for the friends of the Arrow Book Club.

Library of Congress Cataloging-in-Publication Data

Spinelli, Jerry.
The library card / Jerry Spinelli.
p.   cm.

Summary: The lives of four young people in different
circumstances are changed by their encounters with books.

ISBN 0-590-46731-X
[1. Books and reading—Fiction.]   I. Title.
PZ7.S75663L1   1997

[Fic]—dc20   96-18412

CIP   AC

12 11 10 9 8 7 6 5 4 3 2 1   7 8 9/9 0 1 2/0

Printing in the U.S.A.   37
First Scholastic Printing, April 1997

Club edition ISBN: 0-590-13757-3

The display type was set in Eva Antiqua.
The text type was set in Waldbaum.

This book would not have happened without a suggestion from my editor, Ann Reit. I am also indebted to the following: my wife Eileen; my friends Jim and Eileen Nechas; Mike Tucker of the Chester County Astronomical Society; and Cathy Stout, Bob Purrenhage, and Lisa Marple of the Chester County Library.

— *J.S.*

TO ALAN BOYKO

CONTENTS

MONGOOSE

1

Fingers trembling, eyes on the man at the cash register, Mongoose snatched the Milky Way bar and stuck it in his coat pocket.

He waited for lightning to strike. For the hand of God to frizzle him on the spot. The earth to open and swallow him up. Cops at least.

Nothing.

Nothing but himself standing in front of the candy section of the Mini-Mart feeling like a dope. He couldn't believe he was fooling anybody.

"Just look like you're checkin' the stuff out," Weasel had said. "Like you're tryin' to decide what to buy."

Right. So here he was, scratching the back of his head and putting this stupid now-what-do-I-want-to-buy-look on his face. Meanwhile stuffing a candy bar into his pocket.

And nothing happened. The world took no notice.

So he grabbed a handful of Milky Ways and stuffed them. And some Butterfingers. And Almond Joys.

"Bring your coat with the biggest pockets," Weasel had said. It was good advice.

A handful of Snickers. Baby Ruths.

Two aisles over, he could see Weasel's red ski cap bobbing behind the pastries.

M&M's. Tootsie Rolls.

Now the red cap was moving down the aisle, past the sodas and pretzels toward the door.

Time to go.

They met at the cash register. They walked past the man, cool, casual, not looking — ("*Don't* look at him." Weasel had been firm about that) — though Mongoose mightily wanted to.

Outside, the November air splashed cold on their faces, and Mongoose knew he had been sweating. They walked to the end of the block. The moment they turned the corner, as if on signal, they ran, raced up the street, tension bursting into howls of laughter.

They did not stop until they reached Mongoose's apartment house. They went up six flights of stairs and then one more to their favorite place — the roof.

They strutted, they swaggered, they posed. They went to the edge and looked over the town and threw their fists in the air.

"It's ours!" Weasel crowed. "All ours!"

Except for the clock tower of the bank on Main Street, the roof of Mongoose's place was the highest spot in town.

Mongoose, his arm still thrust to the night sky, turned to Weasel and said, "What do you mean, it's ours?"

"Just what I said. If we can walk in there and walk out with half the stuff, we can do anything. Nothin' can stop us." Weasel shouted over the rooftops. "We ain't little no more!"

Mongoose grinned. "Yeah."

Weasel was right. That was the whole point of this night, the new names, everything: *They were not little anymore*. They had both had birthdays — their twelfth — in October, and both had begun to notice the same thing happening. People were smaller, or seemed so anyway. Their teacher, their parents, older kids, grown-ups — suddenly they were not the danger they used to be. And neither were their weapons: detentions, groundings, scoldings, rules, threats.

Nothing and no one was as big or as fearsome as before. They had both felt this, but they had felt it separately, for neither had words to express it.

And then one day in school the teacher called on Weasel during geography and asked him a question about Mexico, and Weasel said, "I don't know."

Now, Weasel was never the greatest student in the world, and he had been saying "I don't know" to teachers for the past six years, seven counting kindergarten. Except he never really *said* it, he mumbled it — "Ahgnnuh" — with his face somewhere down around his shoes. Mumbled it, mangled it — "Ahgnnuh" — so bad it took each new teacher weeks to understand. Substitutes never did.

And lo and behold here was Weasel in November of sixth grade, straight as a drill sergeant, looking at the teacher and saying the same thing, the same thing he had been saying all his life, only now saying it loud and clear as anything you'd hear on TV, proclaiming it: "I don't know."

The teacher, Mrs. Pocopson, blinked and even smiled a little, probably so shocked to hear real words come out of his mouth. Normally when Weasel said he didn't know, Mrs. Pocopson would ask somebody else. This time she didn't. This time she took one step away from the blackboard and said, "You don't know?"

"No," said Weasel, almost calling it out. And then repeating, "I. Don't. Know," stopping after each word. It was as if he had just discovered language. "And I never did."

Mongoose heard snickers. He looked back and forth between teacher and best friend. He had never seen Weasel sit so tall and straight.

Mrs. Pocopson's eyebrows practically shot up to her hairline. She blinked some more. "Is that so?"

"Yeah," said Weasel, "and I prob'ly never will."

Snorts of laughter erupted.

You're dead, thought Mongoose.

But Weasel wasn't dead, only suspended. Mrs. Pocopson sent him to the principal's office, and after catching an earful of Weasel's new lip, the principal sent him packing for two days.

It was like throwing Brer Rabbit into the briar patch. Weasel roamed around town, strewing candy wrappers in his wake, simmering in the juices of a new point of view, *becoming* Weasel. During morning recess on the second day, he showed up at the playground and was mobbed by students. Many wanted his autograph.

On the day that Weasel returned, Mongoose was there when a little kid — a third- or fourth-grader — came up and shook his finger scoldingly and said, "Ouu, Bobby — ." So far Weasel had become Weasel only to himself; the rest of the world still knew him as Bobby Morgan. "Ouu, Bobby — *you* got in trouble. *You* better be good."

Weasel laughed and swatted the kid's finger away. "I don't gotta be nothin'. I ain't even here."

The little kid planted his feet. He glared at Weasel. "You are *so* here."

Weasel wagged his head and grinned. "No I ain't. Not no more." He brushed the kid aside and walked into his classroom, leaving the kid baffled.

Mongoose wasn't baffled. He understood why Weasel had wised off to the teacher. Though he himself did not have the nerve to wise off, he did feel like it. Things had changed, as if he and his best pal had moved to a different place. He wasn't exactly sure where they were but, like Weasel, he knew they were not where they used to be.

That night they had met on this same roof. They had flung words into the darkness and, like fireworks, the words had burst and showered their future with light. They saw the Mini-Mart. They saw spray paint cans. They saw cars. They saw freedom.

And since they were new, they gave themselves new names. Bobby Morgan had become Weasel. Jamie Hill had become Mongoose.

"Why're you callin' yourself a bird?" said the new Weasel.

"It's not a bird," said the old Jamie Hill. "It's an animal. It's quicker than a cobra." Jamie Hill had always liked to think of himself as quick.

2

Now here they were on the roof again, letting their breaths and heartbeats catch up with them.

Weasel unbuttoned his long coat and spread it like bat wings. Mongoose gaped in wonder. "Wow!"

Weasel had folded two pillowcases in half and pinned them to the inside of his coat. They were bulging. It took him ten minutes to lay it all out in neat rows on the roof: Twinkies, Devil Dogs, pies, donuts, cupcakes, coffee cakes. He pulled stuff out of his shirt, out of his pants.

"Okay," he beamed, "your turn."

Mongoose began laying out his loot. Weasel whistled and snatched up a Snickers. "You did good, Goose."

When Mongoose dipped into the bottom of his last pocket, he felt something that definitely was not candy. He pulled it out. It was a piece of paper, stiff. A card. Blue.

"What's that?" said Weasel.

Mongoose squinted. "Don't know." He went to the edge of the roof, where the light was best. "It's a library card," he said.

Weasel screeched, "*Libr'y* card? What're you doin' with a *libr'y* card? Gimme." He snatched it away.

Mongoose shrugged. "I don't know. It ain't mine."

"Ain't nobody's now," said Weasel. He flipped the card over the edge of the roof.

The two best friends sat on the roof, eating their loot, tasting their futures.

Weasel made an announcement: "I'm gonna quit school."

"When?" said Mongoose.

"Minute I'm sixteen. Soon as I wake up. I ain't even eatin' breakfast. I'm goin' right to the principal and walkin' up to his big old desk and I'm poundin' it and I'm sayin', 'I quit.' Then I'll go back to grade school and go to ol' witch Pocopson's class — if she ain't in the boneyard by then — and I'm gonna open the door and turn around and moon her in front of the class."

Mongoose cracked up, picturing it.

"And then I'm gettin' my driver's license. *Then* I'll eat breakfast."

"What kind of car you gettin'?" said Mongoose.

"Firebird, baby. Convertible."

"Ragtop."

"Yeah, ragtop. Red. With mag wheels. Pinstripes." Weasel jumped up. He careened around the roof, his hands gripping an imaginary steering wheel, working an imaginary stick shift. "Rrmmm-*rrmmm.*"

"I'm gettin' a Jag," said Mongoose.

Weasel squealed. "A Jag? That's ugly."

Mongoose shrugged. "I don't think so." He had wanted a white Jaguar ever since he had seen one parked downtown. From that moment on the hood ornament was a fixture in his mind: silver and sleek, the leaping, uncoiling cat.

"White," he said.

Weasel screeched. "White! That's even uglier."

Mongoose bit off a Baby Ruth. He grinned. "Beats your dinky Firebird."

For the next five minutes the two argued over who would beat whom in a car race.

"And after I wipe you off the road," said Weasel, "know where I'm goin'?"

"Where?"

"Back to school. I'm gonna park my red 'bird in front there, y'know —"

Mongoose yipped, "Right next to the bike rack!"

"Yeah!"

They both howled at that one.

"And I'm just gonna sit there with this big grin on my face, and all the little *pew*-pils'll crowd around and beg me for a ride. And old Pocopson'll come along in that ugly old junk heap of hers and I'll be laughin' . . . laughin' . . ." He laughed now, getting a head start. He turned to Mongoose. "Where you goin', after I wipe you off the road?"

Mongoose had never thought about where he would go in his new white Jaguar. In fact, he had never pictured himself driving it. He just pictured the car out there, like a cow in a pasture, waiting for him. "I don't know," he said.

3

The next time they met on the roof, after school two days later, they had spray paint cans. They had bought the paint with money from selling their loot to friends and classmates. Each had two cans, one for practice, one for real. They were practicing on the surface of the roof.

Weasel rose up from his knees and called, "Hey, Goose, c'mere, look."

Mongoose came over. He studied the tall fancy red letters of his pal's signature. He nodded. "Looks good."

"Better than good. It's great."

" 'Cept you can't spell your own name."

Weasel stared down. "Huh?"

"It ain't W-E-E; it's W-E-A. And then it's S, not Z."

Weasel glared at Mongoose. "Yeah? How do you know?"

"I don't know *how* I know. I just know, that's all."

"Why should I believe you?"

Mongoose shrugged. "Don't believe me then."

"I don't."

"Don't."

Mongoose returned to his own signature.

Some time later he said, "You're calling the dictionary a liar."

Weasel's hand stopped. "Huh?"

"That's where all the right spellings are, in the dictionary."

"You saw my name in the dictionary?"

"No, but it's in there. Every word there is is in there."

Mongoose stated this firmly, but Weasel remained skeptical. He scowled accusingly at Mongoose. "You got a dictionary?"

"No, but I heard about 'em. I saw one in school once. You think I'm lyin' about your name, go look in the dictionary, see if I'm lyin'."

Weasel snorted, astonished at the notion. "I ain't lookin' at no *dic*-tionary." He gazed lovingly at his name. "They gonna have to change it, 'cause this here is stayin'."

A thin hiss told Weasel his practice can was empty. He tossed the dead can to the other end of the roof. "Gone home for dinner. See ya tonight. Have your paintin' arm ready." He left.

Mongoose's paint was blue. He was going to get white, like the Jag, but Weasel said, "What if you want to spray a white wall? You can't see it." So he picked blue. He worked on his M till he emptied the practice can.

He kicked the can away and went to the edge of the roof. He could not recall ever being on the roof alone before. Below him lay the town, his world. And how sweet it was to be looking down on it, after a lifetime — baby, toddler, little kid — of looking up. He felt the full power of his years up here, the full power of himself. He drew in a long, deep breath. He felt as if his lungs could expand forever, as if he could inhale every cupful of air from the town, and give it back only when he felt like it.

Something below caught his eye. A small blue rectangle on the ground by the steps leading into the apartment house. It looked like the card Weasel had flipped overboard. The library card.

He went down for dinner.

4

That night after midnight, after the TV glow had faded from most windows, they met at the Dumpster behind the Acme Supermarket. They sprayed their names until the paint ran out. They did not fear being identified, for only they knew their new names.

They wrote their names on Dumpsters and street signs, on steps and walls, on doors and sidewalks. Barely minutes had passed when Weasel held his spray can to his ear and shook it. "Almost empty. One more."

Mongoose shook his can. "Me too."

Weasel said, "I'm climbin'. Somebody wants to see me, they got to look up."

Mongoose watched as Weasel climbed to a roof and signed his name

WEEZEL

on a chimney.

Mongoose felt a thrill for his pal. If it wasn't for what they were doing and the time of night, he would have let out a cheer.

Himself, Mongoose chose a tree. He thought it would be neat to wrap his name around the trunk. He had just completed the third O when he suddenly stopped and drew back in fright. The dim glow from a nearby streetlight revealed that he had just painted over a huge insect. Three times the size of his thumbnail, the bug was now totally blue, even its popped-out beady eyes. Its body was nearly round and appeared to be hard on the outside, like a shell. It was clinging to the tree bark.

Mongoose found a stick and poked at it. It did not move. He poked again. It fell to the ground. Mongoose jumped back with a squeak.

Weasel came over. "What's goin' on?"

Mongoose pointed. "Look."

Weasel whistled. "Man, that's a biiiig bug. Wha'd you do, paint it?"

"Yeah," said Mongoose. "I think I killed it."

"Well," said Weasel, "if you didn't" — he stomped on the bug, making a faint, cereal-like crackle — "I did." He wound up and heaved his empty can. "Let's go."

They went home.

Mongoose lived in a ground floor apartment. He had sneaked out through his and his brother's bedroom window. When he returned he saw, moonlit on the sill, the blue card. He swiped it away. He climbed into his room, stripped to his underwear, and got into bed.

Going to sleep, he thought about the painted bug, the ghostly blue eyes. It occurred to him at last to wonder what the bug was doing there in the first place. It was the beginning of December. It was cold. He hadn't seen another bug in months. As sleep overcame him, the blue beady eyes were beginning to change.

In the morning the blue card was on the floor.

5

Mrs. Pocopson stood tall and stern before the black-board, saying, "I don't like to get into this kind of thing in school, but this time I can't help it. You all saw the *vandalism* on the way to school today. I hope none of you ever disgraces yourself with such conduct. If any of you ever feels the urge to write your name, you come see me." She held up a piece of chalk. "I'll let you write it all day on this blackboard here."

The class laughed.

Mongoose heard Weasel mutter, "Ain't no van'lism."

Mrs. Pocopson turned sharply. "You say something, Robert?"

Weasel glared at the teacher. "No."

Mrs. Pocopson kept staring Weasel down until he turned away. "Anyway," she said breezily, "I know at least one of the *vandals* wasn't my student."

"How do you know, Mrs. P?" someone called out.

"Because the dumb *vandal* doesn't know how to spell weasel!"

The class roared with laughter, except for one.

After school Mongoose and Weasel strolled about town, reviewing their handiwork of the night before. Like seeing your name on a movie sign or in headlines, thought Mongoose. He felt taller. Truly, the town was theirs.

"What now?" he said.

"Hit Mini-Mart again," said Weasel. "Get more paint. Know where my name's goin'?"

"Where?"

"There."

They were walking downtown. Mongoose looked up. Weasel was pointing to the clock tower on the First National Bank.

Mongoose laughed. "No you ain't."

Weasel shoved him. "Ain't I?" He ran to the door of the bank and tried to get in, but the bank was closed. He went next door to the luncheonette. He popped his head in and shouted, "I'm doin' it!"

They took off, laughing, racing down Main.

"Look!" yelled Weasel. He leaped into the street and waved his arms wildly. "Firebird!"

A Firebird — red, ragtop — sped by.

Weasel yelled after it: "That's my car!"

The Firebird beeped.

The two pals ran on, laughing. Life was great.

The boys split, and Weasel went home. Mongoose decided to wander a bit. He checked out every tree trunk he came to, looking for another one of those bugs. In time, he found himself in front of the library.

He had passed the library many times in his life, hundreds, but he had never gone inside. He was not even sure it was for kids.

He pulled the blue card from his pocket. He had put it there after picking it up from the floor that morning. For the first time he took a good look at it. One side was blank. The other side was . . . blank too! He kept turning it over and over. He could have sworn it said LIBRARY CARD when he had looked at it on the roof.

It was just a blue, blank scrap.

And yet still, somehow, he knew it was a library card.

Problem was, he wasn't sure how it worked. He thought maybe it was like a ticket, giving the holder admittance, as to a basketball game. Finding no ticket-taker at the door, he entered, walked up three steps, turned a corner, and found himself facing a counter with a lady behind it.

When the lady looked up and saw him coming, she smiled as if she knew him. Was he supposed to know her? He walked up to the counter and showed her the card. He felt silly showing a blank card. "You collecting tickets?" he said.

She took the card. She looked at it, then into his eyes. The silly feeling vanished. "No," she said, "this is not to let you in. It's to let a book out." She reached across the counter and slid the card into his coat pocket. "Now, how may I help you?"

Mongoose told the lady about the big bug. She nodded and went away for a minute. She returned with a book.

"You'll find what you need in here," she said. She handed him the book. She smiled. "Good reading."

As he left the library, he stuck the book under his coat and in his waistband. He sprinted home.

Only behind the closed door of his room did he take out the book. It was called *I Wonder*. He found what he wanted on page twenty-three. The bug was called cicada, also seventeen-year locust. Mongoose read on. He learned that this cicada bug comes down from the tree as a baby worm and buries itself in the ground for seventeen years. And when it comes out — presto! — it's a big bug that sheds its skin — eyes and all — and that's what Mongoose had found.

Amazing.

Imagine being in the dark — underground — for seventeen *years*.

And when you come out you're different than when you went in.

And then you crawl out of your own skin!

The whole idea boggled him, made him tingly. He looked at his arm. He had goosebumps.

The chair he sat in no longer felt safe. He moved to the floor, his back against the wall. He started paging back to the start of the book — he knew books should be read from beginning to end — but he kept getting ambushed. Pictures and words and numbers drew his eyeballs to them like flies to fly-paper.

He read about a bird that stays in the air for up to four years.

And a fish that climbs trees.

And another bird that fights its enemies by vomiting on them.

And a bird, called the tickbird, that hitches a ride on the back of a rhino.

And an insect — none other than the common old cockroach — that can walk around for two weeks with its head cut off.

And an eel that's electric, that can turn on a lightbulb.

And the mole rat. The book called it the world's ugliest animal, and it was right. He had to spend an hour on the picture of the mole rat alone.

And a worm that can stretch itself up to ninety feet.

Mongoose slid full-body to the floor. The ceiling was spinning, he was woozy.

His mother came in. She frowned down at him. "How long have you been in here?"

"Don't know," said Mongoose truthfully.

"You know you missed dinner four hours ago? You know it's nine o'clock?"

"You know there's a fish that climbs trees?"

Mrs. Hill looked down at her son, on his back on the floor, eyes closed, a look on his face she could not recall ever seeing before. And a book in his hand. About tree-climbing fish she knew nothing, but she did know that if there were such a thing, it surely was not as rare as the sight of her youngest son holding a book. And missing a meal.

"Just letting you know," she said, "the chef's off duty. If you get hungry, make yourself a sandwich."

He made a sound; she wasn't sure what it meant. Carefully she closed the door.

6

"Yo, Goose."

"Say, Weaz."

"What's up?"

"Not much."

They were walking to school a week later, being cool, being twelve.

And Mongoose had just lied. A lot was up. So much was up he was practically twitching. He had finally made his way to the front of *I Wonder*.

He had tried numerous times to read it straight through, but he just couldn't do it. He kept skipping ahead, skipping back, jumping all over the place. Same problem he had with a banana split. Each of its many parts was so tempting, he barely nibbled at one before being lured away by another. Different though, because when he finished a split, he was stuffed, felt like he'd never eat again. With this book, he could wolf it down at breakfast and be ready for more before lunchtime. Wherever *I Wonder* was going, it wasn't to his stomach.

Another difference: banana splits made Mongoose greedy. No grizzly bear ever guarded her cubs more ferociously than Jamie Mongoose Hill guarded a split. But with this book, appetite seemed to move in more than one direction. His hunger was to feed not only himself but someone else, to both take and give, to share. Which is what he did all week to his mother and father and older brother — till *they* were stuffed. But Weasel, he wasn't biting.

And now, on this bright cold December morning, Mongoose had reached the end of his patience. Right there on the sidewalk he grabbed his best pal's arm and said, "Weaz, listen to this."

Weasel frowned. "You look goofy."

Mongoose felt goofy. "You ain't gonna believe this."

"You ain't gonna believe how bad I'm gonna slug you if you don't let go of my arm." Weasel pried the hand away.

"You know that bug on the tree that night?"

"That I mashed?"

"Yeah. Well, that wasn't the bug really. That was just the shell of it, that it crawled out of. And that ain't all. The bug is called a cicada. It's also called a seventeen-year locust, and it's called that because it lives in the ground for seventeen years. Seventeen *years!* And that ain't *all.* When it went *into* the ground, it wasn't a big bug — it was just some tiny *worm!*"

Weasel looked at Mongoose without expression. Mongoose looked at Weasel, waiting for him to say something. He didn't, so Mongoose said, "Want to hear some more?"

Weasel said, "I'm takin' a day off."

Mongoose said, "There's a fish that climbs trees!"

Weasel said, "Gonna sleep in."

"And a anteater eats thirty thousand ants a day!"

"Maybe poke my head out the window."

"Thirty thousand!"

"Laugh at all the baboons goin' to school."

They turned the last corner to school, smack into the blinding sun.

Weasel grabbed Mongoose's sleeve and pulled him to a halt. He moved in front of Mongoose until his face eclipsed the sun. "You with me?"

Mongoose blinked. "And there's a bug that stinks like a skunk."

They walked into school.

All day long Mongoose waited for his chance alone with Mrs. Pocopson, but it never came. At dismissal, in the hallway, he said to Weasel, "Hey, I forgot something. Go ahead, I'll meet you outside."

Weasel looked at him funny but went.

Mrs. Pocopson was erasing the blackboard. Mongoose stood at the doorway. He could not think of how to get started, so he just jumped right in. "There's a fish that climbs trees. And a worm that stretches itself up to ninety feet! And hummingbirds breathe two hundred and fifty times a minute! And I found a cicada shell!"

The eraser stopped on the blackboard. The teacher's head turned slowly. The look she gave him was as blank as Weasel's, yet Mongoose was sure she had heard what he said, was working on it. Suddenly her face broke into a smile warmer and, in its way, more blinding than the morning sun.

He turned and ran.

7

Mongoose dipped the brush into the Planters peanuts can and thought: *Weasel ain't gonna like this. Weasel is* not *gonna like this.*

He had not found Weasel after school that day. But he did find him late that night: at his bedroom window, knocking, waking him up from a sound sleep. Weasel, carrying a gallon can of paint from home — indoor semigloss, pale yellow — a roller, a roller pan, and a small brush, said, "We're goin' to work." Mongoose didn't argue.

So here they were, over in the dark East Side, where streetlights were few and broken windows and empty buildings were many. They had chosen one of those buildings, each taking a wall.

"Goose! C'mere! Quick!" Weasel called from around the corner.

Weasel was standing back from his wall. He waved. "Down here." He walked down to the end of the long, low, brick warehouse. Mongoose followed.

"Now look," said Weasel. He switched on the flashlight he had brought. The beam meandered until it found a wide track of pale yellow, the beginning of the W. It was at the far edge of the wall, against the rainspout.

"Okay, let's go," said Weasel. He began walking, trailing the light along the broad yellow letters

WEEZE

By the time they came to the foot of the L, they were at the other end.

Mongoose was impressed. He looked down the length of the building. "The whole wall."

"The whole wall," Weasel repeated. "Me."

"Never saw one that big."

"Ain't goin' to neither. It's a world record."

They stood admiring for a while. Then Weasel said, "So wha'd you do? Let me see."

Uh-oh, thought Mongoose.

They went around the corner. Weasel trained the light beam on Mongoose's wall, panned across it. Nothing showed but bricks and window holes.

"Where is it?"

"It's there."

The light came into Mongoose's eyes. "Where?"

Mongoose turned away and pointed. "There."

The light beam followed Mongoose's finger to a spot low on the wall, at ground level in fact. There was Mongoose's name, painted in pale yellow on a single brick.

The light fell from the brick onto the ground. Weasel said, "You jokin' or what?"

"No," said Mongoose.

"Why'd you do that for?"

"I don't know. Just did it."

The light splashed into Mongoose's eyes. "You makin' fun of me 'cause mine is big."

Mongoose snatched the flashlight and turned it off. "No. What do I care how big yours is. I just did it, that's all. Maybe I didn't want to waste paint. Maybe this brush you gave me is little. Look." He turned on the light and aimed it at another signed brick ten feet away. "I did three."

Weasel thumped Mongoose on the chest. "You're crazy." He snatched up the Planters peanuts can and poured its paint into his roller pan. Swooping high and low, he painted

MONGOOSE

spelling it perfectly, down the entire length of the wall. He stepped back, reviewed his work, nodded once. He left everything on the ground — paint cans, roller, roller pan — and walked away.

On the way home Weasel talked about quitting school, about his red Firebird ragtop. Mongoose just listened and nodded, packing his silence around a secret. He had not signed three bricks — he had signed four. The fourth was all the way at the far bottom corner of the building, the very last brick. It was so low that it didn't even show. No flashlight, no sunlight would ever reveal it. He had dug dirt away to expose the brick; then, afterward, he had replaced the dirt. It was below ground and would be so forever. On that brick was a name, but not his own. It was

CICADA

8

Rain fell. The air was bitter cold, and the moment the rain touched the earth, it was ice. Then it snowed. Six inches overnight. Then another twelve. Sidewalks became trails, white waist-high canyons.

On one of these trails one night Mongoose bumped into Weasel. Under a streetlight Weasel spread open his coat. Two pillowcases were pinned to the lining.

"I was just comin' for ya," he said. "Time to hit Mini-Mart again."

"Can't," said Mongoose.

"Got to. We're outta paint. Gotta get more stuff to sell."

Mongoose shook his head. "Can't."

Weasel closed his coat. "Why not?"

"Gotta go somewhere."

"Where?"

"The deli."

"Why?"

"My mom."

"What for?"

"Potato salad."

"Potato salad!"

"Yeah."

Weasel grabbed Mongoose's sleeve. "Come on. You can get it at Mini-Mart."

Mongoose pulled away. "She likes the deli's. Gotta go."

Mongoose took off before Weasel could stop him. He headed for the deli, but when he came to it he just walked on by. He turned a corner, doubled back, and soon was entering the public library. He opened his coat and pulled out *I Wonder*.

The same lady was behind the counter, smiling, expecting him, it seemed.

"Here's the book back," he said, holding it out.

She wasn't taking it.

"You gotta give library books back, don't you?"

She nodded. "When you're finished with them."

He held it out farther. "I read it." He added, feeling proud, "The whole thing."

She smiled. "But are you finished with it?"

This lady was getting on his nerves. "I just said I read it."

Her smile went. She fixed her eyes in his. "But are you *finished* with it?"

He stared openmouthed, hooked like a fish on her eyes, her words. It seemed he stood there for days. At last he shook his head. "No."

She smiled. With the palm of her hand she gently pushed the proffered book back to him. "As long as it takes."

Mongoose slipped the book under his belt. He felt silly. "What if it's forty years?"

The lady nodded smartly. "So be it."

As he pushed through the door the cold air and her voice hit him at the same time: "Good-bye, Mongoose."

9

It had been a strange week. For the life of him, Weasel could not figure out Mongoose. They had always been like brothers, even closer. As they met each morning on the way to school, so they had walked together through life, laughing at the same things, wanting the same things (except maybe cars). Now suddenly it was different, as if Mongoose were taking another way, seeing other things.

Like painting his name real teeny on a brick. What was that supposed to prove? Whatever, Weasel figured that was about as weird as things could ever get.

He was wrong.

The strange week had begun the night Weasel knocked off Mini-Mart for the second time. On the way to Mongoose's he had met his pal, and Mongoose had said he couldn't go along, some dumb excuse about potato salad.

Weasel had followed him to the deli — *past* the deli — and on to, of all places, the library. Weasel was seething. He waited, and when Mongoose came out, Weasel lit into him.

"This is a funny-lookin' deli."

Weasel had to bite his lip, the look of surprise on Mongoose's face was so funny. But it wasn't hard to jump right back to mad. "Where's the potato salad?"

"They were out of it," Mongoose tried to say. World's worst liar.

Weasel got into his face. "I followed you. You didn't go to no deli. You came here."

Mongoose didn't say anything. What could he say, caught red-handed? He just looked at Weasel all dumb-eyed.

Weasel hollered, "You lied!"

The point being: You lied *to me.* Sure, over the years they had told their share of lies, both of them. Who didn't? But never had they lied to each other. Till now.

And it hurt. It hurt really bad. Only right then Weasel didn't know he was hurting, he knew only that he was mad, as mad as he had ever been.

So when Mongoose, with that dumb, stupid, guilty look on his face, said, "Ready to go to Mini-Mart now?" — well, Weasel was so mad he wanted to slug him. But he didn't. He just poked him in the chest, kept poking and backing him up until he was flat against the door of that dumb library. And then he said, "You ain't goin' nowhere with me."

And he ran.

And he knocked off Mini-Mart by himself that night, walked outta there bulging like some two-sack Santa Claus. Went home, stuffed the loot under his bed, didn't eat a bite of it, started crying as soon as he laid his head down in the dark, the hurt coming on now. Bit a hole in the pillow.

For two days he walked straight to school, did not meet up with Mongoose. By the second afternoon he had sold the loot and bought four cans of spray paint. And cooled off about Mongoose. He must have, otherwise two of the cans would not have been blue.

Without using the word "forgive" or the word "hope" or the word "forever," he told Mongoose that he would forgive him for lying, cheating, and double-crossing the other night, and that he hoped all this strangeness was gone now so they could get back to being like they had always been forever.

He should have saved his breath.

The next morning, waiting at the corner, he saw Mongoose coming to meet him with tiny, mincing steps. He was counting: "...sixty-six...sixty-seven..."

"What —" Weasel started.

Mongoose scowled and flapped his hand and went on counting. Weasel fell alongside.

"...one *hundred*."

Mongoose stopped and looked back. His eyes grew wide, he shook his head, he whistled. Clearly he was amazed at something. Weasel looked until his eyeballs creaked but saw nothing amazing, only the sidewalk and the fronts of row houses and the crusty, blackened leftovers of the last snowfall.

Mongoose pointed. "See that stop sign."

Weasel said he saw.

"That's where I started to measure. From there to here it's one hundred feet."

"So?" said Weasel.

"That's how long a blue whale is." The way Mongoose said it, you'd think he was praying. "And you ain't gonna believe how much its tongue weighs."

"Aw, man!" Weasel clamped his hand over Mongoose's mouth, thumped him a good one, and shoved him in the direction of school.

Next morning here he comes, walking slow this time, staring down at his hand. As he got closer, Weasel could hear him breathing — fast. *Really* fast. In his hand was a round watch, a stopwatch. He marched right on past Weasel, didn't know he was there, puffing like a jackhammer. Finally Mongoose punched the stopwatch, swayed, tilted, gave Weasel a goofy, wobble-eyed look, and flopped onto a dirt-splattered snowbank.

For a full minute he lay there gasping, like he was dying, worrying Weasel, making him wonder, What do I do? At last Mongoose sat up, looked at the stopwatch, shook his head, gasping syllables: "Two hundred. And fifty breaths. Takes a humm. Ingbird one. Minute." He held the stopwatch up to Weasel's face. "Look how long. It took. Me."

Weasel snapped, "I don't wanna hear it!" He left the baboon sitting there in the snow.

When Mongoose finally straggled into class that day, he didn't even try to hide the fact that he was in cahoots with Pocopson. He just plunked the stop-watch on her desk in front of everybody. He and the teacher didn't say anything, but they looked at each other and traded nods and twinkly little grins, secret little grins.

The chair Weasel sat on seemed to wobble.

10

At dismissal Weasel bolted from school by himself. He wandered the streets, trying to figure it out. What was happening? Where there had been no problem before, suddenly there was. He was in a battle of some kind, without weapons, against an enemy he did not know. All he knew was, he was losing.

The weather had turned warmer, melting snow and ice. At every street corner he had to jump over the cold, gray slush that pooled at curbs and sewer drains. The cold melt quickly reached his socks, his feet.

Every time he passed his spray-painted name on a wall, he stopped and pumped his fist and dared any onlooker to do something about it.

Somewhere along the way he found himself taking tiny, mincing steps and counting:

". . . twenty-one . . . twenty-two . . ."

As he counted on, he began to feel the presence of something, something huge and blue

". . . thirty-five . . . thirty-six . . ."

huge and blue, hovering, looming massively

". . . fifty-one . . ."

Icy wetness lashed across his knees, snapping his breath. He was in the street, and the tire throwing slush was halfway up the block, attached to a red car. Not a ragtop, not a Firebird, but enough to wake him up, bring him to his senses. He grabbed his jeans at the knees and wrung the denim angrily. It was time to stop messing around.

Mongoose wasn't home. Weasel walked the down-town streets, checking out the usual places. Only when he came to the last did he admit there was one place he had been avoiding: the library.

He got as far as the book return bin and stopped. He stared at the front door but could not make him-self go in. A breeze whispered down the street, curled a finger around his neck. The sky was dark-ening toward dinnertime. High school kids were leaving the library.

Weasel went to a side window and peeked in. There was Mongoose, by himself at a big round table. Weasel knocked on the window. Mongoose just sat there, like he was hypnotized by the book in front of him. Other books were spread across the table, like he was taking a bath in books.

Weasel knocked again, louder — and a lady ap-peared on the other side of the window. She didn't seem mad or even surprised to see him there. She didn't try to shoo him away. She smiled and pointed toward the front door and mouthed the words, "Come in."

Weasel stared at her. The breeze was picking up. In a voice not too loud in case the glass was thin, he said, "*You're* telling *me* to come in? You don't tell me nothin'. I go where I want. If I wanted to come in, you think you could stop me?" He laughed and took off.

After dinner he finally found Mongoose at home. He dragged him up to the roof, where things were always good. The wind was roaring in the treetops.

He grabbed Mongoose's arm. "We're gone out tomorra night. And don't give me no lip. We're paintin'."

To Weasel's surprise, Mongoose gave him no lip. He didn't give him an answer either, so Weasel jumped ahead and went for it all. "And then we're quittin'."

Mongoose's eyes went wide. Weasel wanted to laugh. *Take that, blue whale.*

"Quittin'?" repeated Mongoose. "Quittin' what?"

"School. What do you think? I told you I was gonna. You with me?"

Mongoose took a step back. "You said when you were sixteen."

Weasel shook his head. "Too long to wait. I'm doin' it now." Hearing himself say it, feeling it. "You with me?"

The two stared at each other, and then in the howling wind — a *click*.

Instantly the boys dropped to a crouch by the roof wall. They saw the door open and someone step out — a man, a large, hulking silhouette that neither recognized. The man was carrying something. He lugged it to the far end, unfolded it, and stood it on the roof. It had three skinny legs coming to a pyramid point with a fat barrel on top. The hulking figure bent over it.

"Machine gun," whispered Weasel. "Or rocket launcher."

Mongoose was already walking. Emboldened, Weasel jumped out front and called, "Hey!"

The figure unbent suddenly, as if startled, and stood tall above them, broad dark back to them, and a man's voice said, "Hello?" He turned and looked down at them. Both boys jumped back. Weasel screamed.

Facing them was a mask such as they had seen in movies of bank robbers. The only visible face parts were two eyes and a mouth. The mask fit snugly over the entire head like a glove. Then came a pair of earmuffs. Then a pointed red-and-white-striped cap with a pom-pom on the end.

The man chuckled. "Sorry, boys, didn't mean to scare you."

"We ain't scared," Weasel growled, taking another step back.

"In cold weather like this," said the man, "fifty percent of a body's heat loss goes out through the head. Did you know that?"

"Not my heat," said Weasel.

The man nodded, impressed. "Well, when you're my age you'll start feeling the cold. And this will be a cold night. A front is moving in. Snow tomorrow."

Weasel had no interest in weather reports. "What're you doin' on our roof?" he demanded. "That a rocket launcher?"

The hooded head turned Weasel's way. The mouth smiled. A hand patted the black barrel. "This? No. This is a telescope. I'm observing the sky. It's my hobby. There's so many trees around my house, so I asked the manager here if I could come up to the roof. Did you know we're standing on the second-highest point in town?"

"We know it," said Weasel. "This is *our* roof." It was creepy, that mouth, as if the main man were somewhere else and had sent his mouth on up here to talk to them.

"I hope you don't mind," the mouth was saying.

"We mind," said Weasel.

"What're you lookin' at?" said Mongoose.

The mouth made its biggest smile yet. "The Great Orion Nebula."

Weasel and Mongoose said together: "Huh?"

The man pointed to the sky. "See those three stars in a row?" Weasel saw them but was not about to say so. "That's Orion's belt. Orion is a constellation. You boys know what a constellation is?"

Both said, "Yeah," Weasel lying.

"The stars of this constellation are in the shape of Orion, the mighty hunter. So that's his belt you're looking at, the three stars in a row. Now look at the left-hand star, and then down a little from it. See another row of three stars?"

"Yeah," said Mongoose, like he was getting into this.

"Well, the second of those stars only *looks* like a single star to the naked eye. Actually it's a whole galaxy of stars and huge clouds of gas. All together, it's called the Great Orion Nebula."

With rare exceptions, Weasel's vocabulary contained only one question. He asked it now: "So what?"

As he figured, the question stopped the mouth in its tracks. It hung open, dumb, speechless; the eyes blinked.

And that might have settled the whole thing right then and there. The man might have packed up his stupid three-legged contraption and gotten off their roof — except Mongoose, nodding at the spyglass, ruined it all with a question of his own: "Can I look?"

The man backed off. "Sure can. Step up." He pointed. "Just look right in here."

Weasel watched Mongoose step up to the telescope that should have been a rocket launcher. He watched his best pal bend over and peer into the thing.

"You might want to cup your hand around your eye," said the mouth. "Keep away the outside light."

Mongoose hunched his shoulders and cupped his hand; a prayer brushed Weasel's lips: *Please don't let him see nothin'.*

"Right in the center," said the man. "See the fuzzy spot? All those little points of light?"

Mongoose never twitched, was like a statue. "Yeah."

"That's it. The Great Orion Nebula. You're looking at a galaxy, billions of stars. And that galaxy you're looking at is fifteen hundred light-years from earth."

Mongoose straightened up. "What's light-years?"

"A light-year is the distance light travels in one year. It comes to about a trillion miles."

"Wow!"

"Wow is right. But it's no wonder when you consider how fast light travels."

"How fast?" said Mongoose.

"One hundred and eighty-six thousand miles per second."

"What!" gasped Mongoose.

"What!" gasped Weasel.

"Did you say per *second?*" said Mongoose.

The hooded head nodded. "Per *second.*"

Mongoose was face-to-face with the black hood. "Are you tellin' me —" he took off his right glove and snapped his fingers, then quickly snapped them again — "just *that* fast, light goes a hundred and eighty-six *thousand* miles?"

The hood nodded firmly, leaving no doubt.

For a time on the roof only the wind spoke. Weasel thought about his red Firebird ragtop, himself in it, blazing down some highway, asphalt smoking. He did not like this man. With that candy cane cap, he looked like a Santa's elf gone bad. Weasel felt like plucking the cap from his head by the silly pom-pom and flinging it off the roof.

Mongoose put his glove back on and again peered into the spyglass.

"That galaxy you're looking at," said the man, "it's actually moving farther and farther away. It's racing away from us at about ninety thousand miles per hour."

Weasel scoffed, "That ain't nothin'. Soon's I get my ragtop —"

No one was listening.

"It's a big world out there," the man was saying, sweeping his hand across the sky.

"How big?" said Mongoose.

How big? Weasel mocked silently. *How big? How fast? How? How? How?*

The man turned his back and looked out over the roof, the treetops. "Nobody knows for sure."

Weasel went to the other side. "Hey, Goose," he called, "some people comin' by. Come on over, we'll spit bomb 'em."

But Mongoose was somewhere else, calling, "Weaz, c'mere. Look at this!"

Weasel stood at the roof's edge, as he had so many times before. The town — his town — lay before him. Now that's what a roof was for, to look down from, to check out your territory, to feel the size of yourself.

"Weaz! It's the moon! I'm seeing the moon! You won't believe it! It's like I can touch it! C'mere!"

Weasel's heart sank.

Slowly, feeling the cold now, Weasel trudged back across the roof to the door. When he got there, he turned. Mongoose was bent over the gizmo, every part of him hunched in toward his peering eye except one arm, which reached out over the barrel, fingers fluttering, reaching, as if trying to touch the moon.

He hated the man. He hated the spyglass.

He called: "Goose."

Mongoose did not move.

He screamed: "Mongoose!"

With something like relief, Weasel saw the dark form of his friend pull away from the barrel, ready to listen.

"Remember what I said. Tomorra night. I'll come by. Be ready." He did not wait for an answer.

11

The man had been right. Snow started before school let out, and by nightfall it was useless to think about spray painting. The snow didn't stop until lunchtime next day. School was called off.

Weasel hung close to Mongoose all day, lest his pal sneak off to read a book or look through some telescope. They spent the day sledding, snowballing, eating. Mongoose was his old self.

Weasel ate dinner at Mongoose's, then ran home for the paint cans. When he returned, Mongoose was waiting outside, saying, "Where's my cans?" He was eager.

Weasel could have kissed him. "Here." He handed over the two blues.

Mongoose put one in each coat pocket. He held out his hand, palm up. He grinned. "Let's paint!"

Weasel slapped the hand. "Yeah!"

Off they went, laughing, horseplaying, throwing snowballs, two best pals. Just like old times.

The moon, a thin clipping in the black sky, gave little light that night; but all that it gave stayed, puddled upon the sleek surface of the new-fallen snow like rainwater on the hood of a newly waxed Firebird.

Mongoose piped, "Let's do the high school!"

They ran.

Minutes later, standing before the dark, gothic archway, Weasel felt three ways at once. He was thrilled that Mongoose was his old self again. He was shocked at the boldness of his pal's idea. And nervous about doing it. And then he thought: *Hey. I'm never gonna go here. Why should I care?* And felt just one way then: better.

He pulled out one of his cans and gave it a good shake. He stepped through the archway to the thick wooden door that reminded him of a castle. This time he did not write his name. He wrote

I QUIT

He stepped back. "Mongoose, look."

Mongoose was gone. Weasel spotted him around back, trudging past the tennis courts. "Where you goin'?"

Mongoose called, "Football field."

What could Mongoose write on there? The bleachers were covered with snow. The goalposts?

Since he had no intention of ever attending the high school, Weasel refused to honor the main building with his signature. So he autographed other campus sites: the athletic equipment building, the tractor shed, the power plant, the school district offices, parking lot signs. He was signing the baseball field dugouts when he heard Mongoose behind him: "Let's go, slowmo. I finished a long time ago."

Weasel killed his second can, and they headed home. Weasel, wanting to stretch out this good night, suggested they go up to their old spot, the roof.

When they opened the door and Mongoose looked immediately to the sky, Weasel knew he had made a mistake.

Mongoose pointed. "There it is. Orion."

Weasel refused to look.

"How much you think a telescope like that costs?" said Mongoose.

"'Bout half a million, I heard," said Weasel. "You can forget that sucker."

They waded through the snow to the edge wall. They dropped snowball bombs onto imaginary targets six stories below.

Wary of answers, Weasel avoided asking questions. "Tomorra's the big day," he said. "Freedom, baby."

Mongoose, packing snow, said nothing.

"We'll check out the arcade. Play every game. Have us some lunch. Go check out some cars." He poked Mongoose. "Check out some Jags if you want."

Mongoose dropped his snowbomb.

"Wish I could see ol' Pocopson's face, lookin' at them two empty seats."

Mongoose wandered out to the center of the roof and fell backwards, arms spread, into the snow. "Hey, Weaz," he called, "try this. Open your eyes, and all you can see from down here is sky."

Weasel held firm. "So where you wanna eat lunch tomorra? Hoagie Hut? Burger King?"

There being no answer, Weasel rolled a snow-bomb the size of a basketball and lugged it over to where Mongoose lay spread-eagled in the snow. He held the bomb above Mongoose's upturned face. "Hoagie Hut or Burger King? I want an answer."

Mongoose closed his eyes and smirked. "Weaz, what makes you think your mother's gonna let you quit school?"

Weasel didn't know which bugged him more, the question or the smirk. He let go of the snowbomb, but Mongoose, true to his name, was too quick.

12

In contrast to Weasel's mood, the next morning was bright and sunny. This was supposed to be one of his best days ever — no more school! — yet he felt without life, empty.

He knew exactly what he wanted to do. He wanted to march up to Mongoose's and pound on the door and announce: "Who said my mother could stop me?" Making it sound like he had won out over her, like she didn't think he had simply gone off to school early. Then he would grab Mongoose and haul him from his house and they would race for the arcade.

He wanted to, but he could not.

So he decided to perk himself up by checking out his paint job of the night before. He headed for the high school. When he saw the crowds, his first thought was that they were admiring his work. Then he noticed they were gathered around the football field, where he had done no spraying.

The field was set at the bottom of a hill that rose to the top row of the grandstand. Students and even some teachers lined the crest. As Weasel approached, he could hear them exclaiming, see them pointing.

He squeezed sideways through tall bodies until he came out in front. The sun skimming off the snow was stunning, yet he knew at once, as he shaded his eyes, why his pal had been so agreeable the night before and so anxious to paint.

The field was like a page from the world's largest book. In the middle, taking up half the field, was a colossal drawing of a whale, like everything else, traced in blue spray paint. The whale's mouth was open, a blue arrow pointed into it, and a notation in five-foot characters said

4.2 TON TONGUE

Another picture made no sense. It showed a tree with a fish climbing up the trunk.

A third picture looked like a headless cockroach.

Weasel read the rest of the field:

EEL＝VOLTS

HUMMERS DO EVERYTHING
FAST

CENTIPEDE NEEDS 354
SHOES

MOLE RAT — UGLEE!

30,000 ANTS/DAY

186,000 MILES/SECOND

STINK BUG

Giggles and yips of delight erupted all around Weasel. Voices asked, "Who did it?"

Weasel backed away and walked on. He was glad the day was bright and sunny. He wished it would stay that way, that the temperature would go up to ninety degrees and melt every flake of snow, that it would never be night again.

"Hey, Bobby, you're goin' the wrong way."

A kid from school, calling. Weasel walked on.

And saw Mongoose. Coming up the other side of the street, his face buried in a book, not even sensing Weasel. Strolling along, bumping into stuff — *there*, into a mailbox, dumb baboon — his lips moving, some goofy grin on his face.

Right opposite Weasel now.

Weasel stopped. He wanted to call out. He wanted to call across the street that seemed a whole night sky between them now, wanted to call, "Mongoose! Mongoose!" And that would be enough. That had always been enough, just the name.

Jamie!
Bobby!

One would call, the other would hear and turn and come running . . . turn and come running. . . .

But somehow things had changed, and it wasn't enough anymore, just the name. Something else had to be said, and Weasel did not know what it could be, and Mongoose was moving on, walking, reading, up the street, and Weasel did not know and did not care.

He was alone on the glaring sidewalks now. In the cold, clear air he heard a school bell ring.

The town was his.

The Pontiac dealership was on Mayfair. He hadn't been there in a while. He wondered if they had gotten in some new Firebirds. Maybe a ragtop. Maybe red. He felt better just thinking about it. He hoped he could find one with a pinstripe. Maybe a double pinstripe. Mag wheels. *Flames!* Painted right on the hood! Vroooooom! He started to run. He couldn't wait to get there.

BRENDA

Day 1

"Five minutes!"

Brenda froze.

Once, she had watched a TV show about zebras. The narrator said that sometimes a lion gets real close to a zebra and stares at it, and the zebra is so terrified it doesn't try to run. It just stands there waiting to be devoured.

How dumb, thought Brenda at the time. She did not understand the zebra. Now she did. Now an even meaner beast came stalking, ready to pounce, ready to swipe away her very life. And she was paralyzed with fear.

"Four minutes!"

Four minutes. Two hundred and forty seconds.

She squeezed her pillow to her chest. She tried to concentrate on her TV, on the figures speaking and moving, but she could not. The screen was like a half-remembered dream.

When first she heard about it, she had scoffed. Impossible, she said. It would never happen. A date had been set, and a time, but it was so long off it did not seem real. It could not be seen coming down the street. It could not be heard. In her room things were as they had always been. Her beanbag chair. The bed. *Ace Monahan, Weird Kid,* as always on the tube at 6:30 Sunday. She simply could not believe that anything horrible was on the way.

"Three minutes!"

At times like this in the movies, some people would try to look on the bright side. They would say something like, "Well, it's been a good life."

How stupid!

The convict on death row — in the final minutes of a movie or before the commercial — that's who she related to. Sweaty palms clutching cell bars — the raw, terrified stare — the footsteps of priest and warden — the faint buzz that means they're testing the electric chair — the seconds ticking louder, louder — yes, that

"Two minutes!"

she understood. In one movie a man being strapped to the chair cried out, "Just give me one more minute!" How silly, she had thought then.

Her hands and feet were spongy. She was tortured by thoughts that she might have done something to stop this. Had she tried everything? Had she cried? Yes. Pouted? Refused to speak? Refused to eat? Refused to move? Yes, yes, but nothing stopped it. It was a ten-ton steamroller squashing every protest in its way, crunching.

"One minute!"

So fast. She had never known time was so fast. It did not help to remind herself that she was not alone, that it was happening all over town. She had heard once that the greatest fear was fear of the unknown.

"Thirty seconds."

She could hear footsteps now, on the stairs, rising, in the hallway now, closer, on the other side of the bedroom door now . . . the warden, the priest . . . A lock! She should have gotten a lock!

"Ten seconds."

Had it been a good life?

The doorknob turned. She opened her eyes as wide as she could, swallowing, gorging herself on the glowing screen, the beautiful screen.

"Three . . . two . . . one . . ."

The door swung open. Her father walked in. He looked at her. She clutched at the bedspread, she wailed, "One more minute! Pleeeeeese!"

The warden smiled a weak, regretful smile. "Sorry, kiddo," he said and pushed the power button: *plink*. The picture shrank to a point and vanished. Flushed. Gone. Herself with it.

Was it her imagination, or could she really hear ten thousand *plinks* all over town?

The Great TV Turn-Off had begun.

It was 7 P.M. Sunday. Brenda had already done the arithmetic. She would have to go without TV for one hundred and sixty-eight hours. Or ten thousand and eighty minutes. Or six hundred and four thousand, eight hundred seconds.

One week.

At the moment the numbers meant nothing to Brenda. Nothing meant anything. She was numb. Dead.

And so was her beloved TV. The voices, the laughter, the bright leaping colors — gone with the flick of a father's finger. Where moments before *Ace Monahan* was filling the screen, now there was only a flat gray nineteen-inch square. A shroud. A tombstone.

Brenda knew she was in shock. She knew this from hospital and emergency room dramas she watched. Even zebras facing lions went into shock. It was nature's way of shielding its creatures from the extremest moments of agony.

But shock was not a healthy state either — let it go on too long and you might never come out of it. That's why doctors always said of someone in shock: "Keep him warm. Raise his legs." Brenda got under the covers and put the pillow under her feet.

The red numbers of her digital clock said 7:01. Ten thousand and seventy-nine minutes to go. She groaned aloud.

By 7:20 Brenda was starting to come out of shock. And feeling really strange.

Normally she was attached, connected, the stream of light a bright cord tying her to the world within the nineteen-inch tube, feeding her. Now the cord was gone, and she tumbled queasily in space.

She looked around: dresser, bookcase, beanbag chair, lavender curtains. Hanging from the closet door was a stuffed green long-legged frog. Where did that come from? She knew this room must be hers, but it felt like someone else's.

The panic hit at 7:25.

Never, never since the show began three years ago, had she missed an episode of *The Dennison Twins*, not even reruns. And now tonight's show was five minutes from over. What hilarious stunt had the zany, interchangeable brothers pulled this week? Did Robby finally get a date with Heather? Did Bobby mess things up as usual?

Brenda ached to know. The not-knowing became a gnawing sharper than any hunger for ice cream or pizza. She rushed to the TV, she knelt before it. She presented her face to it, chin upthrust, eyes closed, trying to feel on her cheeks some leaking shower of photons, to capture on the nerve tips of her skin some faint electronic tickle of Robby and Bobby Dennison. With cupped hands she reached to the floor as if into a stream, scooping spilled atoms, splashing them onto her face, trying to feel . . . trying to feel . . .

Seven-thirty. The show was over. She had missed it. And now *Pardon My Petunia* was coming on.

Suddenly she could not bear to be in the room. She ran downstairs. She wandered about the house, trying not to think, trying to occupy her eyes. She saw a painted breadbasket on the kitchen counter, geese on the wallpaper, a small hutch in the dining room. The only sound was music from her father's tape player, the same Italian opera guy he'd been playing for years.

He was in the living room. He looked up, smiled. "Lost, kiddo?"

"No."

"You'll get through it. First couple days are the hardest. Best way is cold turkey."

"Not hungry," she told him.

He laughed. "Cold turkey means when you have a bad habit and you totally stop it, just like that." He snapped his fingers. There was a dreamy sadness to his smile. He was getting as goofy as his music.

She sniffed, "I don't have a bad habit," and walked away.

Robby Dennison, that's who had a bad habit: picking his nose in public. If someone caught him, he pretended to be Bobby.

She went out back. Her mother was at the end of the yard, digging with a trowel. Though it was almost eight o'clock, there was dusky light to see by.

Her mother turned. "Hi, Bren. Want to help?"

"What are you doing?"

"Playing with my roses."

"Forget it."

Brenda went back inside. Lorelei Brindamour of *Pardon My Petunia* was allergic to roses. God help the suitor who sent them to her.

She wandered down to the basement, back to the kitchen. She looked at the clock. It was half past *Petunia*. Her father was now singing along with the opera guy. Help!

She went outside to sit on the front steps. She looked up and down the street. A man was watering his lawn. A lady was walking her dog. Two people were jogging. Kids were running. Somewhere a basketball rang against concrete.

She sat up, walked to the driveway, walked to the sidewalk, back to the steps, sat down, got up, went inside, went out back. When watching TV, she would not move for hours, would hardly breathe. It was as if she left her skin, her shell behind on the beanbag chair while her self entered the nineteen-inch world of sitcoms and movies. Now, with no place to go, her self felt like carbonated fizz, like a soda bottle shaken and ready to blow its top.

In the kitchen she opened the fridge — and for a thrilling instant had the light-washed sensation of a TV flicked on. But she faced only jars and Tupperware and such. She spotted leftover onion dip. She spread some on crackers, then finished it off with a spoon. Ditto leftover baked beans. She made a sandwich of baloney, American cheese, lettuce, onion, tomato, pickle, mustard, potato chips. She ate five Oreos with milk. Then two frozen waffles, toasted, with syrup. Then a bowl of Lucky Charms cereal, a dish of fudge ripple ice cream, three maraschino cherries (plus the juice), a carrot, a can of Vienna sausage, a handful of nachos, a banana, and a spoonful of cold mashed potatoes.

She was at the open refrigerator, spoon in hand, when her father yelped: "Brenda! You were in here eating an hour ago. You're *still*?"

Brenda did not know what to say, so she had another spoonful of mashed potatoes.

Her father laughed. "I always heard that when people stop smoking cigarettes they start eating a lot. I guess TV is the same." He took the spoon from her hand. He took the crest of one ear between his fingers, drew very close, and peered into it. "I believe," he said gravely, "you are so loaded it is coming out your ears."

Brenda flipped him a slanted smile. "Ha-ha."

She went upstairs.

She moved as naturally as possible, considering her full load, but once in her room she collapsed onto the bed, groaning. She had eaten through *Bloopermania* and *Maliboo*. *Bottoms Up* was on now. If she could last through that, merciful bedtime would come to the rescue.

After a while she got up and wandered about the room. She stopped at the window and stared vacantly through the blinds. Minutes passed before she realized what she was seeing in the darkness across the street: the telltale bluish glow of a TV screen.

She stifled a yelp. She turned off the light, the better to see. She yanked on the string, the blinds shot up. Yes — it came from the Hurleys' house. And that made sense, because the Great TV Turn-Off was a school thing, for families with children, and the Hurleys were old people whose kids were grown and gone. They lived alone.

She could make out the shape of the screen, a vague movement of shadows. It was maddening, like smelling a pie on a shelf she could not reach.

Then it hit her: binoculars! Her father had a pair. Where? Where? The car! Glove compartment. She raced downstairs, grabbed the keys, ran to the car, got the binoculars, raced upstairs. She threw up the window screen, dropped to her knees, propped her elbows on the sill, raised the instrument to her eyes. . . .

The magnification was shocking. Suddenly she was inside the Hurleys' bedroom. There was the back of Mr. Hurley's head; there was Mrs. Hurley, ironing; there was the TV. It was blurry. She felt for the adjustment knob on the binoculars; she turned it, bringing the screen slowly into focus. She saw a bowling alley, flashing numbers, a cheering audience. . .

She screamed.

She threw the binoculars onto the bed, she pounded the mattress. The Hurleys were watching *Bowling for Dollars.*

Day 2

Next morning, from habit, her eyes still closed, Brenda reached out to turn on the TV. Her groping fingers found nothing but air and the flat surface of the bedside table. Her eyes flew open. The TV was gone!

Her father was in the bathroom shaving. "I took it away while you were sleeping," he explained. "I thought it would be easier for you without the temptation."

"I'm not going to look," she whined.

"Can't is better than won't."

She stomped away.

It was spooky, getting ready for school without *Teen Toons* on, without the set sitting there. The room felt cold. For the first time she realized how much the mere presence of the set had meant to her. There was comfort in knowing that, on or off, it was there. She felt cheated. She would have wanted to touch it one last time, to say good-bye.

At school Brenda expected an atmosphere of gloom and stunned silence, like people being held hostage. She was wrong. The whole place was buzzing about the Great TV Turn-Off. Kids were laughing, bragging about how they survived the first night. Wisecracks flew. It was all a big joke to them.

Brenda was appalled. The school gave out buttons that said *TV — Who Needs It?* She refused to wear one.

From the minute she got home until dinnertime, she ate. Then she ate after dinner. She did her homework for half an hour and ate some more.

Though Brenda loved television, she understood little of how it worked. But she did know that invisible signals sent from TV stations were filling the sky, waiting to be snared by anyone with an antenna and a plugged-in set. She imagined she could faintly hear the signals, her beloved *Bottoms Up* and *The Flirtstones* and *Married . . . With Fleas* whistling like feathered arrows to the blessed homes of people without children.

She knew she had hit bottom when she realized she was willing to watch *Bowling for Dollars*. She grabbed the binoculars, she looked across the street to the Hurleys'. The shades were drawn.

The sun went down. Night fell. The moon rose.

Siss Boom Bimbo

The Magic Pizza

Dude Feud

Show signals hummed overhead. Show signals sang across the stars.

Brenda's father had left behind the rabbit ears antenna to her TV. Brenda opened her window. She held the rabbit ears outside. She closed her eyes. She wiped all thoughts from her mind, made her mind as blank, as ready as a plugged-in TV screen.

Nothing.

She put the base of the rabbit ears in her mouth. She leaned out as far as she could into the night.

Nothing. Not so much as a test pattern.

Day 3

Brenda's mother was at work when she received a telephone call at 9:05 A.M. It was the attendance person from school, ". . . calling to confirm that Brenda is home today. We have no absent request on record."

"That's because she's in school," replied Brenda's mother.

There was silence.

"Isn't she?"

"Not that we know of," said the attendance person. "Her homeroom teacher has reported Brenda absent."

"Oh no," said Brenda's mother.

The person said to stay put and not to worry. She would look into the matter immediately and call back as soon as she had further information.

She called back at 9:50.

"We found her."

"Thank God."

"We think you should come and pick her up."

"Where was she?"

"In a closet."

"A closet? A *closet?* What was she doing in a *closet?*"

"Why don't you come for her now?"

Brenda's mother refused to leave the school without the story. Before dinner that evening, in whispers, she told it to her husband: ". . . looking all over. Couldn't find her anywhere. And maybe they still wouldn't have if some sixth-grader hadn't thrown up his breakfast. The custodian went to fetch a mop from a maintenance closet. It seems that in the same closet was an old broken television. And that's where he found her, spinning the knobs of a dead junker TV set."

Brenda's father drew in a long, slow breath. "Remember when she was a baby? In the playpen? The toy she loved most of all?"

Brenda's mother smiled grimly. "The toy TV."

"Pink plastic."

"She screamed if we tried to take it away."

Brenda's father turned his eyes upward in the direction of his daughter's room. "It's hard to see her suffer like this."

"We'll take her to miniature golf tonight."

The Lives of Annie Fisher
Power Nerds
Moldilocks

Day 4

Brenda knew it was there before she opened her eyes next morning. Even as she slept she felt its presence. It was blue. It was rectangular. It lay upon the table where the TV had been.

She took it with her to breakfast. Her father said, "What's this?" He picked it up.

"Card?" said her mother.

"No," said her father, turning it over, inspecting it. "No printing. It's blank."

"A blank card, then. Pretty color."

"It's nothing. Shall I trash it?"

"No!" said Brenda, snatching it.

Reassured by her daughter's pledge to stay out of closets, Brenda's mother drove her to school. Brenda went from class to class unaware of the stares and whispers around her. Word of the custodian's discovery had spread faster than news of a snow day in June. As one student quipped: "Hey, who needs TV when we have Brenda?"

Like a beamed signal with no antenna to call home, Brenda wandered aimlessly through the day, disconnected from all but the blue card in her pocket. She sensed that the card knew where it was, knew where she was, even if she did not; that as

long as it was with her she could not be flushed away
like her TV picture. The strangest thing was not the
truth of this, but that she did not question it. Every
few minutes she would reach in to touch the card, to
make sure it was still there.

Her mother picked her up after school. "I cleared
myself at work," she said. "I'm going to keep you oc-
cupied till this ordeal is over."

They went to the mall. In the store windows frag-
ments of her reflection appeared and vanished
among displays of shoes and country furniture and
travel posters and stacks of honeyed hams.

They entered Sears. They passed through the
home entertainment department, past an entire
wall of TV screens, all of them turned on. Brenda
faltered. She broke into a cold sweat. Her mother
yanked her onward.

Inside a boutique for women's clothes her mother
shopped for a scarf. Brenda wandered over to a colorful
display of T-shirts. A sign rising from the display said:

What Is YOUR Favorite Color?

While her mother shopped, Brenda stared at the
sign. She knew the favorite color of Harriet on *The
Flirtstones*; it was green, bronto green to be precise.
Shocking pink was the choice of *Pardon My Petunia*'s

comically sexy Lorelei Brindamour. And of course the Dennison twins shared the same favorite color: black.

But what was Brenda's?

Her mother was tugging her along out of the store; she was looking back at the sign, and still she did not know.

Brenda gripped the card in her pocket.

That evening Brenda sat on her bed, dazed. Several somethings were happening at once.

One something was in its fourth day now, over seventy-two hours old. Hardly a minute passed that she did not feel her body turn, like a flower to the sun, toward the table where her TV had been. A confetti of screen moments fluttered without pause through her head. She longed for the soft, explosive puff of the tube as she pressed the power button.

Another something was brand new. She did not understand it, could not even feel the shape of it. It had to do with the sign in the women's boutique, and an especially scary thing that she had begun to notice: the faces of her favorite TV people, as they fluttered through her brain, were becoming less clear, less defined. She found that she had to physically strain to bring the Dennisons' dimples into focus, or Lorelei Brindamour's sexy smirk. With TV gone, the reruns in her head were all she had left, and now they were fading. And she was feeling something she had never known in the warm company of her TV — she felt alone.

For the hundredth time she reached for the blue card. The sense that it would save her had been growing all day. Its connection to her, so strange and unexplainable, seemed at the same time quite natural, as if they had a history together, as if the card had appeared not just that morning but had always been there, on the bedside table. All that had been needed was for the TV to be lifted away, and — poof — there it was.

She went to sleep with the card under her pillow.

Her dreams were of flashing atoms and voices silvery in space. She dreamed she rose from her bed in the night with a feeling that she must go somewhere. She dreamed she went down the stairs and outside. She was walking, walking, until the coolness of a curb edge on the bottom of her bare foot informed her with a start that she was not dreaming at all. She was alone on a dark, silent street. The card was in her hand.

Her feet had brought her to the public library. It was the only place with lights on. She had never been inside before, yet she did not hesitate to enter. That the door was unlocked did not surprise her.

On the front desk under the RETURN BOOKS HERE sign she saw a yellow envelope. She opened it and read:

Dear Brenda,

Welcome home! We've been waiting for you.

Turn left and enter the main reading room. Go to Biography. The shelves are arranged alphabetically. You will know.

The Books

She found the Biography sign. Under it was a round table with a white china plate stacked with crispy marshmallow squares. Strange, she thought.

The bookcases were tall, of dark and heavy wood. At the end of each case a sign declared the span of its contents. The sign on the first bookcase said:

AARON TO BRANDO

The sign on the second said:

BRENDA TO CAESAR

There it was, top shelf, first book: *Brenda*. She had to stand on a chair to reach it. She pulled it down. She sat right there, opened to the first page, and began to read:

Brenda was the four thousandth seven hundred and forty-second baby born on Earth that day. She weighed more than a grapefruit and less than a watermelon. So that he could be present at Brenda's birth, her father Steven gave up the only chance he would ever have to attend a concert of the great tenor Pavarotti. . . .

She read on. About the time she overturned a plate of spaghetti onto her own head. The time she stood up on her seat on the train and sang "I'm A Little Teapot" to the other passengers. The time she put a mud pie in the microwave.

She laughed and she cried as she read, and she exclaimed aloud in the high and echoing room: "Wow!"

On page 9 she read:

Brenda's favorite snack was Rice Krispies marshmallow squares. She ate so many that her parents often said, "Someday they're going to come out your ears."

She went to the round table. She bit into a stickycrispy square. She chewed, trying to remember.

On page 10 she read:

Her favorite color was yellow.

Yellow?

Could it be? She recalled a yellow dress. Yellow pajamas. The yellow crayon so much shorter than the others in her Crayola box.

Yes! It was true. Yellow. She had forgotten.

On page 15 she read:

One day Brenda turned on the television

And that was all. There was not even a period. The rest of page 15 was blank. So was the next page, and the next. The book had many, many pages. She flipped through them all and found not a word, not so much as a page number — nothing but white, empty space.

She inserted the blue card in the page where the words stopped and closed the book. She looked around the reading room. She cried out, "Where is the rest of me?"

The room did not answer.

She heard footsteps.

When the policeman brought Brenda home, her mother could think of nothing to say except, "She's only wearing her nightshirt." As if it were the policeman's fault.

"Yes, ma'am," said the policeman. "That's how I found her. Looks like you got yourself a sleepwalker here."

It was Brenda's father who thought to ask, "Where did you find her?"

The policeman smiled and tipped his hat. "In the library. Good night, folks."

Days 5, 6, 7

In the morning there was no question of school. She ran to the kitchen thrusting keys at her mother, who looked up in amazement, the bread knife dripping marmalade.

"Mall," she said, pulling her mother up from the chair.

She went straight for the women's boutique, to the colorful T-shirts. She stopped at the sign. She addressed it in a voice that turned the heads of sales clerks: "Yellow." She threw up her hands and faced the racks of clothes: "Yellow!"

She led her mother to the home entertainment department in Sears. She trembled to see the wall of TV screens, all showing the same morning hostess biting into the same cherry turnover of the same guest pastry chef. A small group of shoppers was watching. She walked directly to the wall of screens, and for a moment seemed about to walk through them. She stopped and stood before them for a full commercial break. When at last she turned around, she was smiling hugely, a smile her mother had not seen in years. She threw out her arms and proclaimed, "My name is Brenda! I was a really neat little kid. Once I dumped a plate of spaghetti on my own head, and my favorite color is yellow."

One shopper applauded lightly; the others moved on. Her mother could not speak.

For the rest of the day and evening, and the next day and the next, there was no letup. Some places they drove to, but for the most part Brenda wanted to walk, or rather run, as she pulled her mother along like a housebound pup on a leash.

She followed her daughter to the old neighborhood, to the gray clapboard house on Burnside Street, which they had moved from when Brenda was six. She trailed along nervously as Brenda strode into the backyard and began pacing up and down the grass. Brenda crouched and moved branches, peering into the shadows of shrubbery as if searching for lost toys. She knelt before a newly bloomed daffodil. She stroked its yellow petals between her fingers. She closed her eyes and brought the crinkled trumpet to the end of her nose and tickled herself and giggled.

When a white-haired woman with a potholder came out, Brenda bounced right up to her and stuck out her hand. "Hi! I'm Brenda Foster, and I used to live here when I was a little girl. Did you know that this used to be a strawberry patch right here? And over there I buried a mouse with a Popsicle cross on the grave."

The white-haired woman switched the potholder so she could shake hands. She nodded and said, "I see . . . I see . . ." and her uneasy smile relaxed as Brenda jabbered on. Following her young visitor about, the woman every so often glanced at Mrs. Foster with a bemused look as if to say, "What do you feed this daughter of yours?"

It was around noon when Brenda smacked her forehead and said, "Oh man! I gotta go see." She charged into the public library, fairly sprinting back to Biography. Standing on a chair, she pulled a book from the top shelf, opened it at a blue bookmark, scanned several pages, pumped her fist, reinserted the bookmark, let out a whoop — "Yes!" — and charged back onto the street.

This happened every couple of hours for the rest of the week.

They went to the park, to the wading pool where Brenda's mother had taken her as a little girl. Mothers gawked and toddlers yelped in delight as Brenda plopped herself down and launched a splash party.

They went downtown, stopping in every place of business, even law and insurance offices: "Hi, I'm Brenda. My favorite color is yellow." Strangers on the street, clerks behind counters: "Hi, I'm Brenda. My finger is double-jointed. Look!" After dinner they strolled around the neighborhood: "Hi! . . . Hi! . . ."

Brenda made contact with everything. She ran her fingertips over the polished marble of a building downtown. She sniffed an automobile fender, tasted a blade of grass, listened to a black walnut shell, stared and stared at the sky. She felt and smelled and tasted and listened and looked and giggled.

When she wasn't introducing herself to strangers, she was peppering her mother with questions:

"What — ?"

"How — ?"

"Who — ?"

And when she wasn't peppering questions, she was simply talking, jabbering, flinging words with the newfound delight of a two-year-old in a tubful of Ping-Pong balls.

Always returning to the library, to the same book, to move back the blue bookmark, to whoop anew.

On Saturday Brenda's father said to her mother, "What is going on?"

"I'm not sure," she answered. "When I find out I'll tell you."

"She's running you through the wringer. You look like a dishrag."

"That I know."

"But are you okay?"

She touched his hand. "Very okay. Better than I look."

"And her?"

She crooked a finger around one of his. She smiled uncertainly. "Ask me tomorrow night sometime after seven."

Giggling, jabbering, whooping, unflagging, unstoppable — *Brenda?* Could it be true? Her daughter returning after all these years? Is this what happens — this avalanche — when a life suspended catches up all at once? So accustomed to mourning, Brenda's mother hardly knew how to rejoice.

But would it last?

What exactly was this Great TV Turn-Off, this tubeless week? Was it a new horizon truly, or a spell, a bewitching? What would happen come Sunday evening at seven?

She feared trickery. Magic worked could just as easily be unworked, could it not? As Sunday spilled its hours, she watched the clock with growing dread.

And yet when her husband late in the afternoon said, "Shall I put the TV back?" she heard herself answer, "Yes." Because she had to know if it was real.

She spent the last hour in Brenda's room. Brenda herself was gone, disappeared since after dinner. What sort of turmoil was she going through? By eight o'clock, which Brenda would live in this house?

Brenda's mother emptied the box of photos, which she should have put into albums long ago, onto the bed. She shuffled through the prints, searching anxiously for one in particular, one that she remembered above all others.

She found it. She laughed aloud as her own memory precisely matched the moment captured by the camera: Brenda, on the morning of her fourth birthday, standing on the front sidewalk in her yellow pajamas, belting out "Happy Birthday" to herself in case any of the neighbors cared to give her a present. She laughed again and kissed the photograph.

Dopey from exhaustion, she forced herself to stay awake. She dared not lie on the bed.

She touched her daughter's clothes, her things, the Kermit doll on the closet door. She paced. She looked at the photograph. Wherever she turned she could feel the TV, a palpable, weighted presence that funneled all the room's space into itself, like a bowling ball dropped on a bedsheet. It seemed to call, *Look at me . . . Look at me.* She discovered that she was afraid to.

She went to the window. She ran her finger along the blinds. She heard music. Downstairs her husband was playing Pavarotti. How he loved the great tenor. Now he was singing along, earnestly, comically off-key, as usual.

The clock said 6:59.

She turned from the window. Brenda was in the room, one step inside the doorway. She did not seem to notice her mother. She stared at the TV, unblinking, as if frozen. Suddenly she rushed across the room and almost violently punched the power button. Light scrambled across the screen, leaped to Brenda's face as an announcer's carnival voice brayed:

"It's! The! Dennison Twins!"

Brenda's favorite show.

Downstairs, the unlikely duo boomed an aria from *Rigoletto.*

The look of dazed stupefaction on Brenda's face — as if she were not here, but *there* — chilled her mother's spirit. She had seen it so many times before. But then Brenda's hand was snapping out and — *plink* — the picture was off, and Brenda was coming to her, straight at her, hugging her, squeezing with surprising force. "Hi, Mom," she blurted and rushed off.

Moments later there was a distinct change in the music downstairs. Pavarotti was now joined — and quickly overwhelmed — by Brenda's high-pitched bellow, every bit as off-key as her father's: "LALALA LALALA LALALA!" This was followed by clapping and shouts of "Encore! Encore!"

Brenda's mother wobbled down the hallway to her own room, too tired to do anything but smile. She was fast asleep long before her daughter stopped singing.

SONSERAY

1

The man and the boy had been to many places, but the car had been to more.

It was a 1976 Cadillac Eldorado, and by the time it rattled down the street by the abandoned factory, its odometer read 288,910 miles. Side panels shuddered like turkey wattles, silver cord glistened like veins on the skin-smooth tires. Lashed to the chassis with wire, the tailpipe coughed gray sootballs that laid a low, semisweet cloud for half a mile behind.

Rust flakes flew as the car jumped the curb and lurched across the trash-littered field behind the building. It came to a halt before an upside-down washing machine.

"Shoot," growled the man, "somebody's already here."

"Where?" said the boy.

The man pointed. "There."

Fifty yards away, under the middle arch of a gray stone railroad bridge, sat another car.

The Eldorado grumbled under them.

"Ain't we staying?" said the boy.

"Don't know," said the man. "It's up to you."

The boy stared at the car under the gray stone bridge. "What's that supposed to mean?"

"What it says. It depends on you, if we stay or not."

"Why me?"

"You know why."

The boy's eyes were flat and empty. He opened the passenger door. "I know I got to take a leak, that's what I know." He got out and urinated noisily onto a plastic gallon jug.

The man called, "You got to be so loud?"

The boy did not respond. When he returned to the car, he raised his right leg high and drove the sole of his sneaker into the panel above the front wheel. His foot went through the trembling, rusted metal as if it were Kleenex.

"Nice," said the man.

"You gonna turn this thing off or not?"

The man leaned across the front seat. "I'm looking for a job tomorrow morning. If I get one, I want to keep it for a while. Understand?"

The boy flapped his hand at the gathering cloud of exhaust. "Thought you like to save gas."

The man looked at the boy. His shoulders sagged. He sat back up behind the wheel and turned off the key. The Eldorado paid no attention but went on hacking for a good half minute. At last it was still.

2

"Sonseray . . ."

The voice called from his bedroom doorway, drifting in with the smell of grilling bacon from the kitchen, or was it pancakes? He rolled luxuriously into his pillow, stretched himself lazily along his bed. Sundust danced on a teddy bear's nose.

"Sonseray . . ."

He jerked awake, instantly upright, eyes wide, sweeping, searching. She was gone, as usual. Everything was gone — doorway, kitchen smell, teddy bear. The pillow was his own arm, the bed a backseat oozing yellowed foam. Time was, he would have burst from the car and raced down the street, as if he could catch the voice, the face in the doorway. He didn't do that anymore. He was getting older.

Breakfast was on the dashboard. A Baby Ruth. He had not heard Jack get up and leave. But now he did hear footsteps running and squeals and a voice calling, "Stop!" And now there were thumps on the car and two small faces, noses mashed against the windows, staring in at him. He grabbed the candy bar.

The faces, little kids, boy and girl, twisted themselves into goofy shapes and called him to come out. Above them appeared a third face, an older girl. He tore the wrapper and took a bite of Baby Ruth. He made a point of chewing with his mouth open as the little kids screamed and pounded on the window.

He was about to pop the last bite into his mouth when he thought of a better idea: do it out there with them, so they could hear him crunch and chew, so they could watch up close, even smell it. He got out of the car. The three kids backed up, their eyes unsure. The older girl was as tall as himself. The little ones barely came up to his elbow. Runts. The boy runt recovered first, with a scowl on his face and a jaw-jutting demand: "Who are you?"

He ignored the impertinence only because he loved to say his name, especially to strangers: "Sonseray."

"Sonser-*ay?*" squawked the boy runt.

"What kind of name is *that?*" squawked the girl runt.

He had barely thought to answer when suddenly the remaining piece of Baby Ruth was gone from his hand, snatched by the boy who now tore shrieking with his little sister across the littered lot. Knocking the older sister aside, Sonseray took off after them.

Their wagglewhipping rear ends and churning legs gave an impression of great speed, but so tiny were the thieves that Sonseray caught up within seconds. Seeing him behind them, they came to a halt, shrieked even louder, if that was possible, and split, backing off in opposite directions. Sonseray went after the boy slowly, carefully now, for as the boy walked backwards he held the candy bar in the gaping circle of his mouth. Sonseray pointed. "Don't do it, I'm warning you." He held out his hand, palm up. "Give it."

Surprisingly, the boy halted, took the candy from his face, held it out. His wide eyes showed terror: the game had gone far enough. Sonseray reached for the candy, and for the second time it was gone, flipped over his head to the runt sister who ran shrieking the other way.

Sonseray stormed after her, then after him, her, him, as the Baby Ruth sailed back and forth and finally, naturally, landed in the dirt. Would Sonseray have picked it up, dusted it off, and eaten it as planned? Possibly. But he also had the sense, the civilized hesitation to think about it for two seconds. The runts did not. Without so much as a first thought, much less a second, they dove for the candy bar. A swirl of dust arose as they fought and screeched. The candy appeared only once more, in the boy's hand, yellow with dust, then disappeared forever into his mouth.

Sonseray did not see the boy laughing and rocking on his back like an overturned turtle, nor did he hear the girl's howl as she ran to her older sister. He heard only the boil of his own blood gorging through his neck as he picked up something from the ground and headed for the car under the bridge.

3

Even at this distance Jack could see the broken windshield of the other car, and he knew at once what had happened. He tossed the cereal onto the front seat, took a deep breath, and walked across the sun-blasted wasteland.

A woman and three children stopped what they were doing to stare at him. The woman began railing long before he got there.

"Look what he did! Look!" She held up chunks of tinted glass. "What's the matter with him? Is he crazy? It's all over the inside. My children could bleed to death."

The little boy came running, blurting, "He picked up a battery and he went bam, bam, bam! There's glass everywhere! Is he crazy?"

The little girl spouted, "We could bleed to death!"

The older girl was picking glass from the car floor. The way the kids were dressed, you never would have thought they lived in a car. Jack wondered how long they had been here.

The mother wore a green T-shirt and baggy tan khakis. Her fingernails were broad and crusty as a trench digger's. She stood before him. "I don't leave them alone, the little ones. Never." She shook her head adamantly. "I know where these kids are every minute of every day. *And* night," she said pointedly, as if expecting a challenge. "If I'm not with them, Hilary here is. These are well-behaved children. Supervised. Normal in every way."

Jack was tempted to turn around to see if there was a judge or social worker behind him. Instead he nodded. "Yes, ma'am. And I'm sorry about what happened."

The little boy snarled up at him. "Sorry don't cut it, pal."

"Tyler, shut up!" the mother snapped. Turning back to Jack, she said, "You can't let your son run wild like that. What am I going to do now? There's no window."

Jack wanted to say, He's not my son, he's my sister's son. He wanted to say, My sister died from a drug overdose three years ago, but I took over the kid long before that. Then I lost my job at the ice cream plant and since then we've been in fifty towns and everywhere we go he gets in trouble. He goes wild and does something and we have to get out. He wanted to say all that, but what he really said was, "I got a job today. I'll get you a new windshield. Till then I'll get some plastic to put over it."

He headed back to his car. He could strangle that kid. So mean, he was. The temper, the rage always simmering underneath. His mother was never mean. Weak, yes. Confused, messed up, dreamy, dumb — yes — but never mean. And quick, the kid was. Didn't waste time getting to know you. He met you, he hated you. Just like that.

As much as anything, it was the kid who kept them in the car. Jack got a job almost everywhere they went, but he had to wait a week, maybe two, for his first paycheck. Then they could rent a room somewhere, give the car a rest. But half the time they never got that far. The kid would get in trouble, and off they went to the next town.

Back at the car Jack treated himself to a handful of cereal. The market had had his favorite, big plastic no-frills bags of Cheerios-looking stuff. For a buck nineteen, it was as good a bargain as you could get. Of course, the kid hated them, would rather starve than eat them, didn't care that they were cheap. Typical kid that way, money meant nothing. Poor as he was.

Jack had to admit that sometimes even he got a little tired of the fake Cheerios and was tempted to buy something more expensive. Then he would think of how the kid hated them, and he would buy them for spite.

Before going to look for something to cover the windshield, he took another handful of cereal.

4

Sonseray saw it all.

After demolishing the windshield, he had walked around town for some hours, itching for more windshields. Returning, he broke into the factory for a look around. Which wasn't easy, the windows being clapped over with plywood. There was just enough light to see that there was nothing worth seeing. Crummy, trashy floors that creaked and echoed as he walked across them. Emptiness, darkness. Even the dog turd he stepped in was dead, a sawdust cake.

He went upstairs. With his trusty foot he kicked a hole in plywood, and sunlight poured in like milk from a bottle. He saw her at once. In all the panorama before him — the Eldorado below, the other car, the railroad bridge, the whole litterscape, the trees, the rooftops, the sky beyond — his eye locked instantly on the woman at the other car, though at that distance he could cover her with his fingernail.

The mother.

Without taking his eyes from her, Sonseray lowered himself to his knees and rested his hands on the sill, his chin on his hands. The freshly broken plywood smelled fruity. He watched her walk from the other side of the bridge back to the car. She carried a small cardboard box. He knew what she was doing. She was picking up the thousand pieces of glass that he had made, putting them into the box and carrying them off, dumping them in a safe place at a safe distance away from her children. That's what mothers do, protect their children.

As she neared the car, he saw her flap her hands at the two little ones, shooing them away. He smiled, he nodded. Yes, yes, act mad, scare them away from danger. She was doing it right, doing it perfectly. The boy kept running back, challenging her, disobeying. Sonseray whispered, stirring dust on the sill, "Holler at him." And she did, she did! He could hear her voice, even hear the crossness in it. He hungered to be hollered at.

Later he saw Jack go over and get a good hollering for himself.

5

"Why?"

Jack hated himself. For years he had been asking

that question, and for years the answer had been the same: "I felt like it." It was futile, it was stupid. A thousand times he told himself, Don't ask, Don't ask, and here he was, because the first time brought no answer, asking yet again:

"Why?"

"I felt like it."

Yeah, well, he felt like doing something too, but murder was against the law.

It was dark. He could hear the kid eating in the backseat. Whatever it was, it smelled good. Beefy, cheesy. The kid always ate well, always had money. While Jack waited for his first paycheck, the kid would be living like a king, stuffing his face.

"I had to go buy plastic at a hardware store. It cost a dollar thirty-nine. You know how much food I can buy for a dollar thirty-nine?"

The kid snorted. "Yeah, ten bags of that dog food."

"It's Cheerios. And it's good." He took another handful to prove it. "I told you not to do nothing. It's the first thing I said, before I ever shut the engine off. Don't do nothing, I said."

"And I did something."

"That's right," and he almost said it again — *Why?* — but caught himself.

"I disobeyed you."

"That's right."

"You gave me an order and I disobeyed. I turned around and did just the opposite."

Jack said nothing. He was being mocked, his own oft-uttered words thrown back at him, and as usual he was late to realize it.

"Someday you're going to take off and leave me behind like a stray mutt. You'll be in the next state before I know what hit me. That'll teach me."

Jack grinned in the dark. How this kid could take words of genuine fury and make them sound silly was a mystery.

"A stray mutt."

Jack almost laughed. He stuffed more fake Cheerios into his mouth to keep it busy.

The kid tossed his paper and plastic out the window, then followed them into the darkness. Within seconds his footsteps were swallowed by the orchestra of insects. No sounds came from the other car, the little kids quiet at last. Even here, bedtime was bedtime.

Jack woke up when the kid returned, slamming the door, not caring. It seemed hours later, with the moon high on the windshield, when the voice came from the backseat: "Did she roller-skate?"

She.

Jack's first reaction, as always, was surprise. Maybe once a month, at most, the kid would ask a question about her. That was it, one question a month. And naturally, with the silence stretching and stretching in between, Jack came to assume that the kid had forgotten, was giving it up. So by the time the next question came, it seemed to pop out of nowhere.

And yet, in a strange sense, not out of nowhere. The fact that he never said "my mother" — only "she" — and that Jack always knew instantly who "she" was told him that, no, it did not come out of nowhere.

Did she roller-skate?

Hah! No was the answer, but hardly the story. How about, Did she *try* to roller-skate?

He could remember it like yesterday; actually, better than yesterday. He and Noreen had found these old-time metal skates, the kind you clamp onto the bottom of your shoes. Two pairs in somebody's trash. So they put them on and off they go, first time for both of them. And Jack's rolling down the sidewalk like he's been doing it all his life, when he hears this crash and scream behind him and veers onto somebody's grass to stop and look, and there she is, off the curb and into the street and halfway under a parked car. Laughing.

That was the thing: laughing. She picked herself up and just like that was down again. And that's how it went: Jack sailing up and down the street while Noreen bounced from car to pole to pedestrian like a pinball, the both of them laughing, but Noreen especially, laughing like she couldn't get enough of it, laughing like he'd never heard her since. Just about the best day of his life, now that he thought about it.

Did she roller-skate?

Jack knew the question would never be asked again. It would stay shiny and new, rustless as a showroom Cadillac, for years if need be, until answered.

Still, he wasn't helpless, for there were answers, and there were answers. And the power of delay was his. About the only power he had, it was, and he used it, holding back on the answers, and the stories he could tell this boy about his mother. Before the craziness, the rebellion, the drugs, the overdose. Jack was the only one left who remembered her as a kid, and maybe it was there even then, but what did Jack know, he was only a kid himself, and if his sister woke him up one morning by wrapping a worm around his toe, well, hey, that was just Noreen.

He could tell the kid about the time she punched a boy in the nose, or the time she painted the grass red, or the night she and Jack snuck out of the house and caterwauled like alley cats outside the window of a neighbor. He could ramble for hours, for days, and don't think he wasn't tempted. But why should he? What had the kid ever done for him? Did the kid ever offer to share his food? Did he ever say thank you? Ever apologize for being a traveling volcano, for losing Jack jobs in seven states?

So Jack doled out the answers one word at a time, one per month, and received in return some small, grim satisfaction that in one area at least he held the upper hand, even if the kid didn't know it.

Did she roller-skate?

He waited a little more, then delivered his answer at last into the darkness.

6

"No."

Sonseray thought of it as a jigsaw puzzle, thousands of pieces spread out in front of him. Each piece was a memory, or a question already asked or waiting. If the answer was yes, two pieces fit together; if no, the piece went sailing. There were many more question pieces than memory pieces. Only a few fit together so far, giving teasing, disjointed glimpses. A little red-haired girl on roller skates would not be one of them.

Sometimes he wanted to ask all the questions one right after the other, take up a whole day, a week if need be, not even eat. But then he would be distracted, would catch sight of a mother still going strong — he could spot them a mile off — yanking her kid along, or snapping "Put that back," or just being by herself. Oh yeah, even the ones alone. If the kid wasn't with them, they were on their way to pick the kid up. From the minute they left the kid off somewhere, the rest of the day was nothing more than a long U-turn back to pick-up. Guaranteed. They carried the smell of *kid* wherever they went.

And they were everywhere, the mothers. They reached into the cupboard in their kitchens and pulled out their credit cards in the supermarkets and drove their cars and jogged in pink-laced sneakers. The world was full, stuffed, overrun with mothers. They were common as dirt, and more rare than a fifty-cent piece in the gutter. He loved them and he hated them, and he hated their kids. He hated their smugness. He hated most of all those moments in a mall, outside a toy store, when the kid would hold something out to his mother that he no longer cared to carry and would say — no, command — "Hold this," or maybe not even hold it out, maybe just dump it into her bag and say nothing and not even look at her, his trailing hand leaving the thing behind as the rest of him was already tearing into the store. And the mother takes the thing, accepts the thing — what else, she's the mother. And

Sonseray would want to yell at the kid in the store: "Hey, don't be so smug. I'm not as alone as I look. I got one of them too, ya know."

But of course he didn't. He hadn't had one since he was ten, when she died, somewhere "two hundred miles north of Chicago," he was told. And hadn't lived with one since he was five, when she left him with Jack, who then had a job and a wife. And it was feeling bad about that that drained away his wanting to ask a thousand questions. And it was remembering, Hey, wait, but I really did have one once, that encouraged him now and again to ask a solitary question. That and, like yesterday, the sight of a girl on roller skates.

No.

He sent that puzzle piece sailing.

7

He could not believe it. After all that happened yesterday, here they were again, back at the car, the mouse droppings, poking their heads in the one open window. The smell of dream bacon curled one last time through his mind and was gone.

"Hey, Soopadoop, come on out and play."

He closed his eyes against bright sun. "The name's Sonseray."

They pounded on the car. "Hey Sillydilly! Hey Soopypoopy!" They howled at their own wit.

Where was the older sister?

It wasn't the name calling that finally brought him out of the car; it was the braying, pipsqueak voices that he knew would never allow another second's sleep. They stood by the upside-down washing machine, the boy pest waving something in his hand. "Look what I got and you don't."

Sonseray yawned and stretched. "What?"

"A hockey puck. I found it. Ha-ha." He turned around, stuck out his softball-sized rear end and waggled it. The girl pest did the same.

Sonseray started off toward town.

He heard them run after him. "My mom says you're crazy," snarled the boy, suddenly not so playful. "She says you're a lunatic."

"You don't belong on the streets," snarled the girl.

"Yeah. You oughta be locked up."

"You oughta be in a cage."

"Yeah!"

"Yeah! And you know what else? Huh?"

They were walking backwards in front of him, their heads jerking forward with every word.

"You're a bum!" shrieked the boy.

"A bum!" yowled the girl.

"A bim boom bumbitty bam boom bum!"

They were rolling on their backs in the yellow

dust, and the older sister was coming now, running, calling, playing mommy, "Leave him alone!"

Mirth made the runts careless. Two steps and Sonseray was above the boy. He snatched the hockey puck from the tiny hand and started walking. Instantly they were at his legs, clawing and squalling, but then the big sister was pulling them off, and the noise died out as he walked on. He tossed the puck away.

Miles, minutes, meant little to Sonseray. He knew only that he walked for a time and came to a shopping mall. He went in.

At Hickory Farms a pudgy, black-haired lady smiled when he stopped at a platter of bratwurst samples. A dozen dice-sized pieces sat impaled on toothpicks. The lady nodded approvingly as he plucked one up and dipped it into the little white bowl of sweet mustard. She giggled as he captured the sample delicately between his front teeth and withdrew the toothpick with the flourish of a swordsman. Her eyebrows went up, awaiting his opinion. He tilted his head, closed his eyes in thoughtful chewing. He swallowed, he nodded: "Good." She beamed.

By the fourth or fifth sample she was no longer beaming. After the twelfth, as Sonseray for the twelfth time nodded and pronounced, "Good," she

stared coldly at the empty platter. And then when
he, with a devilish grin, plunged his finger into the
mustard bowl, she reached out instinctively and
smacked his hand. Off he swaggered, so pleased
with himself, licking his finger, just another rude
teenager. She carried off the plate and contami-
nated bowl to the back. When she returned with re-
placements, she noticed him three shops down, just
standing there, staring at her. She wondered if she
should call security.

Sonseray roamed. He did not like this kind of
mall. It was fake. It pretended it was outdoors, with
its trees and long-tongued plants and the sky showing through glass panels in a vaulting roof. Indoors
should be indoors, should feel indoors, with box-
shaped rooms and walls and ceilings that you can't
see through.

Mothers were everywhere. Strolling the glossy
black corridor floors, shopping the stores, waiting in
checkout lines, resting on benches. All wore either
sandals or sneakers. He especially liked the ones
with brightly colored socks.

A few had their kids by the hand, but in most
cases the kids had no physical attachment to their
mothers. And yet, as Sonseray knew from countless
hours of watching, an attachment was there. Except
for the occasional toddler who would walk all the
way to Cleveland if you let him, the kids seemed

tied to an invisible string that kept drawing them back like yo-yos.

He listened. As some people listened for bird calls, Sonseray listened for mothers. All about him he heard them: directing, snapping, soothing, threatening, promising, yessing, noing, wait'll-we-get-homing.

Behind him one of them called: "William — here." Sonseray turned. He began walking toward the voice, making his way through the shoppers. It was a game he sometimes played. As the mother's scanning eyes landed on him, the real William rushed into her. As her arms received him, her eyes stayed with the teenage boy coming toward her, staring so directly, so boldly. Sonseray waited until the last step, the mother's eyes widening, before veering off, having sniffed, having tasted.

Teenage girls came racing down the corridor. "Mom!" they yelped, shoes squeaking as they pulled up to a woman in a satiny, lavender jogging suit and a lavender ribbon cinching her ponytail. The taller girl was beside herself, pawing at her mother. "We found them! There's two left. They're only thirty dollars."

The lavender mother kept walking, scanning windows. "For two?" she said.

The girl screeched. "No, Mom, for one. But that's nothing. They're on sale. Can we get them now? You said. *Please!*"

Sonseray, standing before a soft pretzel shop, whispered to himself, "We'll see."

The mother patted the frantic girl on the head. "We'll see," she said and walked into a card shop.

The girl behind the counter in the pretzel shop was rolling out ropes of dough, cutting them into foot-long lengths, looping them into pretzels. Sonseray picked one up and flung it past the startled girl. It smacked into the glass door of the oven, where it sagged like the body of a wall-whipped snake.

Farther down the hall Sonseray entered a toy store. He walked up and down the aisles. By the time he came out he had broken the legs off a plastic ironing board, cracked three toy cannons in half, poked his finger through too many plastic package windows to count, and pulled the heads from two dolls, one of which squawked.

A display of paperbacks, their covers gaudy as jungle birds, caught his attention in a bookstore window. He halted for a minute, staring, then rode the escalator to the second floor, walking faster now. He scooped up a handful of sand from a trash-and-ashtray stand and dumped it into the coffee cup of a lady sitting outside a cinnamon bun shop. He plucked the baseball cap from a sandy-haired head and Frisbeed it over the railing down to the first floor. He kicked the bulging shopping bag of a teenage girl and swiped an ice cream cone from the hand of a little kid. Shouting erupted behind him. The mall music stopped and a voice, seeming to come from the glass-paneled sky above, said, "Code nine . . . code nine . . ."

Back on the first floor, he whirled through a video arcade, punching buttons, jerking joysticks, sending the place into an uproar. And then, outside a dollar store, he saw the scene that, if he waited long enough, he always came across: boy, mother, a moment of smug contention. The boy was holding a small white plastic bag out to her, he was whining, "You hold it." She was saying, "It's your stuff. You hold it."

Nothing made Sonseray's blood boil more. He swooped past them, snatching the bag from the ingrate's hand. He whirled, came back and growled into the kid's shell-shocked face, the kid's head snapping back as if punched: "You little jerk."

It was time to run. Behind him he heard the mother's footsteps: defending her cub. She would step in front of a cement truck to save him. He loved her for that, and as he burst through the door and into the parking lot, he had to fight the impulse to turn and rush into her arms. Five minutes later he was half a mile from the mall, strolling down a bright sidewalk bordered by crewcut lawns and yellow pansies.

8

He walked to town. He was not hungry, but he was hot. A sign above a bank said the temperature was 98 degrees. The sun was almost directly overhead. Shadows were short.

He turned abruptly and pushed through a glass door. Coolness washed over him. The Eldorado's air-conditioning had died twenty towns ago.

"Feels good, doesn't it?"

Was the voice speaking to him? He realized he was standing with his eyes closed. When he opened them he saw a woman behind a counter. There were books on shelves behind her. To her left were more books. Through an archway he could see round tables where people sat, some reading newspapers, and rows of book-filled cases, like a battalion at attention. He was in a library.

"Hit a hundred yet?" said the lady, smiling. She was old, judging by her almost-white hair, though her voice when his eyes were closed had seemed much younger. Strangely, he had no sense of whether she was a mother or not.

"Ninety-eight," he replied.

The lady kept smiling at him. He stood just inside the door.

"Stay awhile?" she said.

He shrugged.

"Have a card?"

"Huh?"

"Library card. Do you have one?"

"No."

"Want one?"

"No."

He felt time drop him and fly on with only his voice receding: *Nonononononononono...*

When time picked him up again he was at the counter. "You sure?" the smiling lady was saying; she was holding out her hand. He gave her the white plastic bag he had taken from the boy. He hadn't realized he still had it.

"Are you sure?" she repeated slowly, her voice twinkling, as she turned the bag upside down. Out fell a box of crayons, a Spiderman ring, two speckled jawbreakers and a pack of baseball trading cards. She pulled the wrapping from the cards.

"Are . . . you . . ."

She turned the cards over, one at a time — baseball faces, baseball caps, until one was left, the bottom card.

". . . sure?"

It was unlike the others. No face, no cap, just plain blue. She held it before his eyes, she smiled. "This is it." She reached across the counter and slipped the blue card into his pocket. She nodded toward the reading room. "Make yourself at home."

He thought of leaving, but instead followed her directions. He walked through the archway. For an instant, crazily, he thought he smelled bacon.

He meandered among the round tables and the tall bookcases. He did not touch the books. He admired the glassless ceiling. He heard a faint voice. He kept looking to see who was speaking, but the people at the tables had their heads down. He knew two things about libraries: they had books, and you weren't allowed to speak in them. Three things: in summer they were air-conditioned.

The voice seemed less distant near a second archway at the far end of the great room. A sign said CHILDREN. He followed an arrow down a stairway. The voice was coming from behind a closed door. A hand-lettered sign propped on an easel said:

TODAY!

PRESCHOOL

"MISS STORYTIME"

1 P.M.

9

When Edwina saw the boy open the door, she assumed he had made a mistake and would be gone. Instead he came right in. Family emergency, she thought, he's coming for one of the mothers. But no, he simply took a seat. Had to be at least in his teens. Sullen face. Could use a bath too. And a haircut.

By now of course she was reading to a dozen backs of heads; the preschoolers having turned to stare at the creature slouching in the back row. Was that his intention, to disrupt Storytime? Or was it just general teenage boy mayhem?

As the mothers swiveled their children's heads back to the front, Edwina turned the page and read on. Though she was an unpaid library volunteer, she took pride in her professionalism. Once she donned her blue-and-gold silk robe and became Miss Storytime, nothing — no crying child, no late arrival, no unwelcome visitor — could turn her from her task of reading to the children every Wednesday at one.

A squeaky voice yelped from the audience: "Miss Storytime!"

Once, in an identical moment, Edwina had put down her book, looked at the child and said, "Yes?" but there had been no answer. In the following years it happened many times — "Miss Storytime!" "Miss Storytime!" — and Edwina had come to understand that these were simply the spontaneous outbursts of children who could not contain the thrill of finding themselves in the same room with her. Now when it happened, Edwina raised one eyebrow in responding salute and read on.

Was he here to mock her? This was always possible with teenagers.

She finished *Babar* and began *Madeline*. The boy was sprawling, stringy-haired head lolling drunkenly to one shoulder, eyes closed, heels propped on the seatback before him, arms flopped over flanking chairs: in short, the typical arrogant I-do-as-I-please teenage boy slouch.

Maybe he was running from the police. Who would think to look for a delinquent in a preschool story hour?

Was he sleeping?

She read the final lines:

"And to her surprise she found
That suddenly there was enough hound
To go *allllll* around."

She showed the last page and dramatically closed the book and bowed. Applause showered her warmly. As usual a tiny voice or two yipped, "Don't stop,

Miss Storytime!" but the mothers were already moving, chairs were sliding, and in a minute they were gone.

The boy remained.

What was she to do, alone now with a slouching teenager twice her size, a murderer for all she knew? She wanted to run. She wanted to stuff her story-telling robe into her tote bag and get out of there. But her hands were not moving, and neither was the boy, and the fourth book continued to lie insistently on the table.

Every week the librarian left three books on the table, three picture books to be read. This week Edwina had found four. But the fourth was clearly a mistake. It was not a picture book but an adult paperback, a dingy, cotton-eared romance titled, now that she glanced at it, *Love, Call Me by My First Name*. There was a carousel rack of them upstairs in a corner, and that's where this one certainly belonged, with its typical cover of busty, blousy, long-haired voluptuine and her swarthy adorer.

The sloucher, whose crusty, propped-up sneaker soles obscured his face, was not sleeping. Somehow she knew this, as she knew that the paperback on the table was in fact not a mistake. From some dim distance she heard the little ones — at least *they* looked up to her — belt out the chant that began every hour: "Miss Storytime, Miss Storytime, read us a story!" Her trembling fingertips idled along the gold threadwork of her silk robe and at last reached for the book.

She began to read aloud.

10

She did not believe it. The clock on the wall said ten minutes to five. But it was true, her own watch said the same. She had been reading for almost three hours.

In all that time he had moved only once. She had seen it between his sneaker soles: one eye, suddenly wide open, then shut again.

And now, as he unslouched himself and made his way toward her, she wanted nothing more than to plead, "Please, stay, I want to go on." To show him, she kept reading: ". . . watched from the doorway as Sonseray rode off, then ran to the dormer window on the third floor to keep him in view as long as possible, for every time he left she —"

He finished the sentence: " — feared she would never see him again." He reached out. His mouth had a shape she could not identify. Tears were in his eyes.

She handed him the book.

11

So it was real after all. Even the cover he remembered. Not that he had ever forgotten, but in recent years it had begun to seem too much like a remembered dream, story and mother both.

In how many libraries — a hundred, a thousand — had he scanned the shelves for the cover, the title? How many bookstores, drugstores? Wherever they stopped and sometimes where they didn't, making Jack screech to a halt, bolting from the car to check out a Rite-Aid or Thriftway. Until, lately, he had despaired of ever again finding the book, and of finding in some measure the mother who had read it so many times to him when he was little and did not know that she was not forever. He had begun to think he had dreamed himself up.

He tossed the blue card onto the counter. The librarian said nothing. He knew — she knew — the book would not return.

Walking, he opened the book and picked up where the lady in the robe had left off. It was all coming back to him, the story of Rebecca, who lived on the seacoast high in the pines, and the mysterious man on a horse. The book was half over before Rebecca said to him, "Have you a name, sir?" and his mother would stop reading and look at him with that grin and her face all waiting for the answer, and he would say, making his voice low and grown-up, "I have, madam," and his mother would read as she had a hundred times before, "And what might that be, sir?" and she would wait again and he would blurt out, "Sonseray!"

Sonseray.

Him. Himself. His mother. Noreen Molarski.

While other four-year-olds nightly begged for tales of red dogs and green eggs, of big bad wolves and little engines that could, Sonseray craved *Love, Call Me by My First Name*. It was the only story his mother read to him, and all he wanted. He never had to beg.

It both tickled and frustrated him that no matter how many times his mother read the story, Rebecca and Sonseray did not seem to know that the ending would be happy. They wanted to be together desperately — his mother would gasp out the word: "*desss*-peratelah" — but the whole world conspired to keep them apart. Complications, enemies, misunderstandings, bad luck — such a tangleball! — would it ever unravel?

It did, every time, in the last chapter, Sonseray and Rebecca rushing into each other's arms, galloping off in the foaming surf. And always on the last page, the sweet tip of the story, himself allowed to bite it off while his mother swooned and fluttered her fingertips over her heart. . . .

He stopped walking. He leaned against a street sign pole. There was traffic but few buildings. Across the street a hand-painted sign on white plaster said RAY'S AUTO REPAIR. There were no curbs. His shadow leaned halfway across the roadway. Ray, back pocket disgorging a rag, was working late.

He closed his eyes and pressed the book between his hands and chest. In time he felt the thumping but was unsure of the heart's location. Out of Ray's came the explosive chatter of an air-powered nut wrench; he smiled, seeing the dreamy drumming of his mother's fingernails on her breast. To the passing cars, to the long shadows and Ray the wrencher, and to his mother, who gave him the gift he could never lose or run away from, to her dreamy, quirky, sad and silly face, he recited aloud the final words of his favorite and only bedtime, daytime, lifetime story: ". . . and just before dawn, as Sonseray held tight to her hand, Rebecca gave birth to a baby boy."

APRIL MENDEZ

1

When my father said we were moving to a farm, I thought to myself, Okay, good. I was sick of the toilet that would never work. Sick of seeing my breath in winter in the bedroom. Sick of being afraid to open the kitchen cupboard because a rat might jump out, like it really did once.

So I was happy to come here, to a farm in Pennsylvania. Until I found out what kind of farm it was.

A mushroom farm.

I always hated mushrooms. In New York City that was easy to do: I just didn't eat them. I don't eat them here either, but I can't stop breathing, and that's where they get me. Because they stink.

Well, not the mushrooms themselves, but the stuff they grow in. It's not regular dirt, like any decent, normal plant. Oh no. They have to grow in poop. Horse poop to be exact.

There's piles of it all over. Heaps. Mountains. You can see the smell steaming off it. My father's boss laughed the first time he saw me holding my nose. It's only part poop, he said (except he said "manure"). He said they mix it with corncobs and other stuff. Big deal. They could mix it with Peppermint Patties and it would still smell like poop.

"Don't think of it that way," my mother tells me. "Think of it as the opposite. A perfume." She lifts her upper lip, sticks out her little finger, and says like a French lady, "*Eau de perfoom.*" I laugh, and still smell poop.

Now, do these mountains of horse dung stay outside where they belong? Oh no. The workers shovel it inside, into long low buildings, because that's where mushrooms like to grow. In the dark.

In spite of their taste, in spite of the smell, maybe I could stand to live with mushrooms if at least they grew in the sunshine like everything else. But they don't, and that makes them creepy, evil, the werewolves of the plant world. Sometimes I think they're in cahoots with the moon. Sometimes at night I feel them out there in their long low houses, silently oozing their little round white faces up out of their dark, smelly blankets: the moon and her million babies. I get the willies.

"It's your imagination running away with you," says my mother. Maybe so, but the stories I hear around here don't help either. Weird stories about mushrooms and their dark powers and how they can grow *anywhere*, wherever it's dark and there's the smallest speck of dirt. I had a nightmare once that I awoke to find them sprouting from between my toes.

So I never have to be told to take a shower; instead, I usually have to be told to get out. I try to keep my dark places lit up. I lie outside on a blanket in my bathing suit. I keep my arms upraised, I make sure both ears get a turn at the sun, and I spread my toes apart with jelly beans.

I don't think it's going to get better when school starts next week. I hear they call people like me "mushies."

Maybe I could stand all this if there was a library around. In New York City the library was only two blocks from our apartment. Whenever I felt bad, that's where I went. In fact, I went there when I felt good too. I was there every day. I got mad one time at Christmas when I found out the library was closed.

I loved my library card. It was all creased and smudged and spilled on, and the corners were rounded and furry. But it was the only official card I have ever had, and the reason it was so beat-up was because I carried it with me everywhere, because I never knew when I might need it. My mother said it was a good thing I had it too, letting me bring books home, because otherwise I would never leave the library, because I couldn't stop reading. She would have to bring my meals to the library and send along my stuffed red hippo so I could sleep right. We used to laugh about that.

I still have the card. Each day I stick it in my pocket, just like in New York City. But I'm in Mushroom Land now, and I haven't seen a library since we moved here.

2

When I woke up this morning a breeze was blowing *eau do perfoom* through my bedroom window. I knew I needed a break.

I decided to pack a lunch and take a hike. Then I figured, why wait till lunch? I put a cream cheese and jelly sandwich and an apple in a paper bag and announced to my mother what I was doing. I told her I would only go as far as the trees at the edge of the farm; you can see them from the house. She said take something to drink. I said I'm not going to be gone that long. She said be careful.

It was true — I didn't think I would be gone very long. I didn't expect to go past the trees. But I got there so fast, I thought, What kind of hike is that? And I could still smell the smell. So I took out my sandwich and kept walking. I guess my idea was to keep walking until I came to the end of the smell.

I walked through a field of cornstalk stubble, jumped over a little stream, climbed some fences, crossed some more fields, more mushroom farms, and always, steaming on the horizon, were the ever-present dark brown hills of *perfoom*. I finished the sandwich, finished the apple, and was starting to wish I had brought something to drink when I came to a road. I turned onto it.

I hadn't seen another person, and only a couple of cows since I left my house, and the road was just about as lonely. Every few minutes a truck roared by, and that was about it. It seemed like the rest of the world was smart enough to stay away from this place.

Mushroom Land is sort of hilly. The road dipped out of sight ahead of me, so I heard the next truck coming before I saw it. When it did come into view, it wasn't a truck after all, but a bus, green and white. I don't know why, but I stopped to watch it, and as it barreled down the road toward me I thought I must be having some kind of hallucination, those fumes were finally getting to me. Because I imagined I saw a word painted in big white letters across the green stripe above the wide window of the oncoming bus, and the word was

BOOKS

And then I jumped into my own hallucination. I was standing in the road waving my arms like a banshee, the bus blowing its horn and veering out to miss me, not slowing, not stopping. And then it was past me, gusting in my face — a bus without windows on the sides — and then brakes were screaming and gasping and half a city block beyond me the bus came to a halt, its two right wheels deep in blue roadside flowers. The squared-off top swayed against the sky.

I ran for the bus. A side door opened, someone came out — a girl, about high school age, hair dark as mine but longer, stomping toward me, yelling at me: "You're not hurt, are you? Huh? Are you?"

She had a little silver ring in one nostril, and another through one eyebrow, not to mention a bunch in her earlobes and on most fingers. I couldn't talk. I shook my head. I cringed. I thought she was going to trample me. She grabbed me by the arm and started dragging me to the bus.

"Are you lost?"

I couldn't take my eyes off her fingernails. Every one was long as a dagger, every one was a different color, a different design.

"Well?" she demanded.

"No," I said.

It occurred to me to resist, but I kept thinking of the word in big white letters. So I let her hoist me onto the bottom step of the bus. The driver was a lady with a baseball cap and a T-shirt picturing a whale. She swiveled her seat to face me in the doorway.

"Are you all right?" asked the lady.

"I will be," I told her, "if you get this fiend off of me."

The girl poked me from behind. "Wha'd you call me?"

I took a swing at her and missed. I wasn't afraid now with the lady there. "Knock it off!" I yelled.

The girl laughed.

The lady reached out and touched my shoulder. "What are you doing out here by yourself? Why were you waving us down?"

I told her about the hike and about looking up and seeing that word coming at me. "After that, I don't know. What kind of bus is this?"

She smiled and took my hand and pulled me all the way in. "It's a bookmobile."

I turned to my left. I was looking down an aisle to the back of the bus, and on both sides were shelves crammed with books. I had read about magic buses and giant peaches and flying couches. Maybe this wasn't a hallucination after all; maybe I was smack in the middle of a story.

I kept staring down the aisle. "Is this real?"

"As real as you," the lady said. "Have you never seen a bookmobile?"

"I never *heard* of one."

I took one step forward. I reached out and touched a book.

"We make stops all around the county, mostly in rural areas that don't have a library nearby."

"Okay, o-*kay*," Miss Wondernails snapped. She grabbed my arm and started dragging me out of the bus. The lady grabbed the other arm, and for a minute I thought I was going to be wishboned.

The lady shouted "Let go!" so suddenly and so loud that I jumped and the girl let go. The lady pulled me closer to her and said to the girl in a voice just like my mother uses when she's had enough of me, "You can do what you want, but I am *not* going to put this child back on this road by herself."

They stared at each other for a long time. Only the girl's eyes looked fierce now; the rest of her had sort of slumped. Then she lunged past me and jabbed a glitter-sprinkled purple fingernail in the lady's face. "You get me there," she snarled, "you hear?"

Like she was turning a page, the lady moved the purple dagger aside with her own ordinary-looking finger. "Don't point," she said. "Close the door."

The girl yanked the door shut and tromped down the aisle to the back.

"What's going on here?" I asked the lady.

"We're being hijacked," she said. "Have a seat."

3

There was an extra seat up front, but I was too itchy to sit. I went to the back. The girl was sitting on the floor, bridging the aisle, her back against one bookcase, the bottoms of her feet up against the other.

"You're the hijacker?" I said.

Her eyes were closed. "You got a problem with that?"

"I was never hijacked before. You got a gun?"

A smirk crossed her face. With her eyes still closed, she pulled something from a little leather pouch hanging from her belt. It looked like a tiny homemade hatchet. The handle was maybe three inches long. The cutting part was a razor blade. Now she was looking up at me.

"Would you really do it?" I said.

"Do what?"

"Hurt somebody?"

Suddenly the blade swiped in front of my face, just missing my nose. She grinned. "What do you think?"

At the very back of the bookmobile was a small table. I sat on it. It seemed like I should be afraid, but I wasn't.

"What's your name?" I said.

"What do you care?"

"Are you always so grumpy?"

The driver called back, "Her name is Nanette."

Nanette sent a "Shut up" up the aisle.

"My name starts with A," I said. "Want to know it?"

"No."

"It's a month."

"I said no."

I chuckled. "Well, you can already figure it out. You know it's not August, right?"

She stared straight ahead at her own shoe tops.

"The fourth month." I leaned down toward her. "After March?" She glared up at me. "April."

If I didn't know it couldn't happen so fast, I would have thought she hated me.

"Want to know my last name?" I said.

Out came the razor blade; it was turning in front of my eyes. "Try it."

The bookmobile slowed down.

"Okay," I whispered. I leaned back real slowly. She put the razor away.

The bookmobile speeded up.

I kept my mouth shut for as long as I could. Finally I said, "Mind if I ask why you're hijacking us?"

She was back on the floor, eyes closed, head against a row of adult paperback mysteries. "Yes," she said.

Suddenly I noticed something. "Hey, look at the shelves. They're tilted!"

Every shelf that I could see was slanted downward away from the aisle.

"So the books don't fall out when I take corners on two wheels," the driver called back.

"Whoopee," said Nanette.

"How old are you?" I said.

"Ninety-five."

"I'm eleven and a half. Did it hurt getting those rings put in?"

I kept asking questions, and she kept not answering.

"Do they get caught in stuff?"

"Does it bother you when you blow your nose?"

"Do you have others that aren't showing?"

Then, when I said, "Can I touch one?" the reaction was different. She didn't say anything, she didn't nod, she didn't even open her eyes; but her shoulders moved just a tiny bit and she gave a sniff, and somehow I knew it wasn't a no.

I let myself down from the table. I got down on my knees beside her, facing her. With her purple eyeshadow and long black lashes and the silver rings in her eyebrow and nose, she looked like an Egyptian princess to me.

I reached over and with just the tip of my finger I touched the one in her nose. I pushed it from vertical to horizontal. "Wow," I whispered. Her breath brushed my fingers. I gave the ring a tiny tug; the side of her nostril puckered. "Does that hurt?"

"No."

Then I touched the one in her eyebrow. Then I started touching her fingernails. Her hands were lying limp in her lap, all ten nails facing up. One thumb had a skull and crossbones; the other was pink with a white heart and a Cupid's arrow and tiny pink letters that said

N.M.

L

W.P.

I lifted one of her hands, just the fingers, just to feel such fingers. I expected her eyes to come flying open, but they didn't.

"Are you N.M.?" I whispered.

"Wouldn't you like to know."

"How about W.P.?"

She smirked.

"Your boyfriend?"

Her eyes were open, staring at me. I couldn't tell if she was mad or not. She called up front, "Hey, when's that stop coming up?"

"About two minutes. Stiller's Corner."

"Then my stop is next."

"Yep. Dorcas Road."

Nanette gave a sharp nod. "That's me. That's where my life starts. I walk out that door, I'm born." She jumped to her feet and wiggled her hips, she clapped her hands and threw them in the air. "I'm a newborn baby!"

She was transformed. She was happy, perky, goofy. She did a funny dance up and down the aisle. I had to laugh.

She didn't calm down until the driver called out "Stiller's Corner!" and the bookmobile came to a halt.

Within seconds we were mobbed, mostly by kids, but a couple of grown-ups too. The driver swiveled around, and the table behind her became a check-in/checkout counter. The littlest kids found their books on the bottom shelves; the older kids' books were higher.

Nanette and I sat on the table in the back. I felt giggly, watching it all. I wanted to dive in and splash in books. "Don't you love libraries?" I gushed.

She looked at me like I was a poison mushroom.

"Ready for my last name now?" I said.

"You ready to die?" she said, putting her hand on the leather pouch.

I jumped down from the table and mingled with the books.

4

A half hour later, as we were pulling away from Stiller's Corner, Nanette said to me, "Ask me again who W.P. is."

She was back on the floor. I sat down cross-legged, facing her.

"Who's W.P.?"

"Walt Pintero."

"Who's Walt Pintero?"

"My fiancé."

"You're getting married?"

"You better believe it."

I guess I was staring at her ring finger, because that's about the only place she didn't have one.

She held out her hand, spread her fingers. "He'll probably give me the ring tonight. Maybe tomorrow. He wrote to me." She pulled a piece of paper from her pocket. It was lined and folded many times down to a small cube. She held it against her cheek and closed her eyes and smiled dreamily. "Meet me on August twenty-fifth at eight o'clock at night. Usual place. We will get married."

Today was August 25th.

"What's the usual place?" I asked her.

She grinned. "Only the shadow knows." She wagged the paper cube in my face. She put it between her lips and stamped it with her bright red lipstick. "Rising Sun," she said.

"Huh?"

"That's where I'm going. That's where the usual place is, where we meet at eight o'clock *to*-night." She kissed the paper cube and stuck it back in her pocket.

"I thought you're getting off at Dorcas Road," I said.

"I am," she snorted. "Because that's the closest this junk heap goes to Rising Sun. So I have to walk the rest of the way. Because the stupid driver —" she cupped her hands and shouted up the aisle "— because the stupid driver won't drive me there!"

"Tell her why," the driver called back.

"Because the driver is stupid!"

"Because if I miss my stops people will call the county library, and before you know it the police will be looking for us."

Nanette stuck her tongue out up the aisle. "I don't care," she said. "I'm going to meet my honey. I'd walk a hundred miles." She held her nose, she honked, "Eewww, there's that smell again. You people got a lot of skunks down here."

"It's not skunks," I said, "it's mushroom soil. It's what they grow the mushrooms in. Horse poop."

She stared at me. She looked a little queasy. "I love mushrooms. I eat them by the handful. And you're telling me they grow in poop?"

"Horse poop."

She threw up her arms. "Oh, oh well then, good, *horse* poop. Great. For a minute there I was afraid it was *kangaroo* poop. Now I feel better."

I'm pretty sure she was kidding.

"So how do you know all this?" she said.

"I live on a mushroom farm."

She nodded and stared at me, like she was recording my answer.

"I wish I didn't," I said. "I hate it. Sometimes I think about running away."

"I didn't just think about it," she said. "I don't think. I do."

I laughed. "Hey, you can't say those words yet. You have to wait till you marry Walt Pintero."

She rolled onto her back along the aisle floor. She threw her hands to the ceiling. "Walter! Walter!" She jumped to her feet, grabbed a book, held it open in one hand, and played the role of preacher: "Nanette, do you take this man to be your lawfully wedded husband . . ."

She went through the ceremony, taking all three parts, making her voice low for Walt and the preacher. When she came to ". . . I pronounce you man and wife; you may kiss the bride," she made a little mouth of her thumb and forefinger and kissed it. She kissed it real long, with her eyes closed, and for a second the bookmobile was a chapel and the tilted bookshelves were pews crowded with relatives on either side of the aisle.

"I'll throw rice!" I said, and I stood on the church steps and showered her and Walt with handfuls of rice as they walked down the aisle and out into the bright sunlight, beaming and laughing and waving to the crowd.

"Dorcas Road!" called the driver. The bookmobile slowed to a stop.

5

Nanette and I stared at each other. For a moment I had the feeling that she didn't want to stop, that she wanted the ride and the spell to go on forever. I know I did.

I looked up at her. "Do you have to go?"

Her eyes fluttered like purple butterflies. "You kidding? I got a date in Rising Sun. Eight P.M."

"The usual place."

She nodded. I think she wanted to touch me, but she turned and walked up the aisle.

I couldn't just let it go like that. "Nanette!" I called. She turned at the door. I ran, reaching into

my pocket. "I have to give you a wedding present."
She was on the lower step. "It's my old New York
City library card. I know it's a stupid present, but it's
all I have. Maybe someday when you're in New York
you can pretend you're me and get a book out."

She was shaking her head and pushing my hand
away when the driver said, "Take it, Nanette. It's her
best thing."

Nanette stared over my head at the driver. The engine rumbled under us. Then she took the card from
my hand and put it in the same pocket with Walt
Pintero's letter. I watched her walk away.

Behind me I heard the driver's voice: "Have you
gotten any mail since you moved to Pennsylvania?"

"No," I said, watching Nanette.

"Don't you just love to get mail?"

"I do."

"She'll need your address."

I called, "Nanette! Nanette! Come back!"

Nanette stopped but didn't turn. She just
slumped. In her heart she was already in Rising
Sun. She did not want to come back. But she did,
scowling at me.

From over my shoulder a ballpoint pen slipped
into my hand.

"Nanette, you have to write to me. I didn't get one
letter since we moved here, and I love to read letters

even more than books." I balled my fists and crouched to show her how sincere I was. "Will you write to me, pretty please?"

She just stood there, totally disgusted with me.

"I'll give you my address," I said. "Give me the card."

She gave it, but it wasn't my old library card. It had the same size and shape, but it was brand-new, it was blue, and it was totally blank on both sides. "Where's my card?" I screeched.

Nanette dug into her pockets. All she came up with was Walt Pintero's letter.

"I don't believe you lost my card already!" I was crushed.

"They're waiting at the next stop," said the driver.

I glared at Nanette and began to write on the blank card. She snatched it. "No last name."

"Okay, okay," I said. I snatched it back and printed my first name and address and handed it to her.

"May I go now?" she said sarcastically to the driver. She didn't wait for an answer.

From the bottom step of the bookmobile I watched her walk down Dorcas Road. I waited until I figured she was at the limit of my voice. I cupped my hands to my mouth and shouted as loud as I could: "Mendez!"

Her hands shot to her ears, but I knew she was too late.

6

The moment we started up I said to the driver, "Was she really hijacking us?"

The driver smiled. "She wanted to believe she was. But I don't think you and I were in any danger."

"What about the razor? Weren't you afraid?"

"The razor wasn't for us."

I stared at her. Something told me not to ask the next question. "Who was it for?"

"The only person she would really hurt."

I could hardly get the word out of my mouth: "Herself?"

The driver nodded. "She showed me the scars on her wrists. I'm afraid she wasn't kidding. That's why I went along with her."

I just stood there, holding onto the back of the driver's seat, watching flecks of hay fly off the farm truck ahead of us. The flecks got blurry.

"Who *is* she?" I said after a while. "What's her last name? Where is she from?"

The driver shook her head. "Where is she going is the question. She needs a future."

Suddenly the gloom vanished. "Her fiancé! Walt Pintero! They meet at eight o'clock tonight. They're getting married." I pictured Nanette at that very moment, somewhere along Dorcas Road, tossing away the leather pouch and running all the way to Rising Sun, to the usual place, right into Walter Pintero's arms.

The driver snorted. "Don't count on it."

From the phone on the bookmobile the driver called my mother to tell her where I was. She gave me orangeade from her thermos. I asked her how she knew the library card was my best thing. "Lucky guess," she said. During her lunch break she drove me right to my front door.

7

There were pumpkins in the fields — at first I thought they were basketballs — when I got my first letter from Nanette. It said:

Dear April — or is it September or January?
I know its a month.

He wasnt there. Not that you care or anything but you said you wanted some mail (not MALE — thats for me which I didnt get) so nice terriffic wonderful person that I am Im sending you this letter. I waited til the place closed up. I came back the next morning and waited til it closed up again and the next day and the next. Not that I care its just I dont like somebody standing me up after I walked all that way. Actually hes a jerk I shuder to think I almost married him. Im lagh lauf laffing can you hear me? "HAH HAH" because Im thinking to myself (ha! who else would I think to?) what am I doing? Im telling all this stuff to a 11 year old what does she care? So here Okay? heres your letter. Dont say I never did nothing for you. Seeya. Have a nice life.

Nanette (the hijacker)

I read her letter a hundred times. I felt bad that she was stood up by Walt Pintero. I cried when I remembered her dancing in the bookmobile. But the thing that bothered me most about the letter was how it sounded — like she would never write to me again.

But she must want me to write back to her, I thought, because she had put a return address on the envelope. So I did. I told her I was sorry about her fiancé. I asked if she had gotten any new rings. I didn't talk about my own problems, I figured she had enough of her own. I just put "Nanette" on the envelope. I still didn't know her last name.

One week went by, two weeks. I didn't hear from her. I wrote to her again. Still no letter back. Then, the day before Thanksgiving, I got three. And not only that, they were fat. Three fat letters.

I ran to my bed, I tore them open. I could hardly believe my eyes. Most of the words I couldn't even read. It was more scribbling than writing, slashes of ink from one end of a page to the other, inky round stab holes in the paper. On the Friday and Saturday after Thanksgiving, I got five more fat letters. I couldn't understand a word, not even my own name.

I spread the pages over my bedsheet. They covered the whole thing. It was like one of those modern paintings that don't look like anything. I stared until the inky slashes ran together into one big smear through my tears.

I kept thinking of the scars on her wrists, and the leather pouch hanging from her belt. And the driver's words: *She needs a future.*

I folded the letters and stuffed them in my pockets and carried them to school and everywhere else I went. I walked under the trees at the edge of the farm and whispered her name. I looked in the direction of Dorcas Road. I wished I could make her happy again. I wished I could give her a future.

After days of wishing and walking, all I gave her was a letter. I was afraid to say anything about the unreadable ones she had sent me. I was afraid to ask how she was doing. So I just stuck to myself:

Dear Nanette,

They call me a mushie in school. I was going to tell you I don't care, but I guess I do. I don't have a lot of friends, just a couple of other mushies. I hang around the school library a lot. Sometimes outside the school when the wind is blowing, the other kids hold their noses and point at me and go "Eewww!" I am surrounded by mushrooms and horse poop. I spend a lot of time daydreaming about running away.

Your friend,
April

The minute I mailed it I started kicking myself. What kind of monster was I, dumping my troubles on somebody who couldn't even handle her own? I hated myself.

Her reply came four days later. I could read it.

Dear Mushie,

You run away and Ill call you that 4ever.
MUSHIE!   MUSHIE!   MUSHIE!
Plus Ill kill you besides. Dont be a jerk.

Nanette

PS Mushie

I didn't know whether to laugh or cry, so I did both. In my next letter I told her how much I miss New York City. I told her I knew I was too young to really run away, but I couldn't help thinking about it.

Her next letter was longer. Again she called me names and threatened me. Then she said:

Get off this missing stuff. You wont see whats in front of you. Ill tell you what. If you stop missing NYC Ill stop missing You-Know-Who. Deal?

I told her it was a deal.

She told me she lives with her aunt and uncle. She said she was sorry for the pile of unreadable letters. "I must have been nutso there for a wile," she wrote. She signed the letter Nanette McSorley.

I asked if she had any friends in Rising Sun.

She said funny I should ask that:

My aunt saw me crying one day and said what you need is somebody to talk to. And I said I already have somebody.

8

We write about twice a week now. I don't talk about running away anymore. I complain sometimes. I ask a lot of questions. She tells me about her new job at a hair salon. She repeats my questions and then she answers them. Sometimes the answers are pages long. I never knew anyone who takes answering so seriously. Sometimes I wonder who is giving who a future.

We sent Groundhog Day cards and valentines, and we just did St. Patrick's Day.

Speaking of cards, she said she's sorry about losing my old library card. She said as a memorial for the card and me, she carries the blue one with my name everywhere she goes.

We have a plan. I sent to the county library for the bookmobile schedule, and I've already picked out the date in June, two days after I get out of school. I'll bike to the nearest bookmobile stop and hitch a ride. Meanwhile, Nanette will already be on her way. Maybe she'll have enough money for her own used car by then, but she'll walk if she has to, she says. We'll meet at Dorcas Road.